Hope's Healing Love

Crooked Arrow Ranch, Book 2

Jenna Hendricks

Books by Jenna Hendricks

<u>Triple J Ranch</u> –

Book 0 - Finding Love in Montana (Join my newsletter to get this book for free)

Book 1 - Second Chance Ranch

Book 2 – Cowboy Ranch

Book 3 – Runaway Cowgirl Bride

Book 4 – Faith of a Cowboy

Book 5 – Cowboy Blessings

Book 6 – The Cowboy's Game

<u>Big Sky Christmas</u> –

Book 1 – Her Montana Christmas Cowboy

Book 2 – Her Christmas Rodeo Cowboy

Book 3 – Her Mistletoe Cowboy

Book 4 – Her Sleigh Ride Christmas Cowboy

<u>Crooked Arrow Ranch</u> –

Book 0 - Wounded Hearts Ranch (join my newsletter to get this free)

Book 1 – A Broken Heart Mended

Book 2 – Hope's Healing Love

Book 3 - Love's Healing Balm

<u>Standalone Novels –</u>

Christmas Crazy in July

See these titles and more: https://JennaHendricks.com

Book 3: Council of Magic
Island of Misfits
Book 0: Island of Misfits
Book 1: Coming soon
Chronicles of the Fae Princess –
Trilogy Published by LMBPN Publishing
See these titles and get their links at <u>https://www.jlhendricksauthor.com/</u>

Contents

Newsletter Sign-up

Do you love clean & wholesome contemporary cowboy romance? Want more? Then check out Finding Love in Montana today!

By signing up for my newsletter, you'll not only receive this book, but a couple more free stories as well!

If you want to make sure you hear about the latest and greatest, sign up for my newsletter at: Subscribe to Jenna Hendricks newsletter. I will only send out a few e-mails a month. I'll do cover reveals, snippets of new books, and giveaways or promos in the newsletter, some of which will only be available to newsletter subscribers. (https://jennahendricks.com/newsletter/)

JENNA HENDRICKS
TRIPLE J RANCH
Finding Love
in
Montana
A Triple J Ranch Prequel

When there is hope in the future there is power
   -- Zig Ziegler

Prologue

Harir, Iraq

One year ago

"See the columns at the top? How they are marked by the alphabet? Then on the side is a number." The blond-haired Army officer spoke to the four local women taking his class via an interpreter. While he had picked up some Arabic, he did not know the local Kurdish language other than "hi" and "thank you."

He was stationed in the Kurdish province of Northern Iraq on a joint US base filled with men and women from various branches of the US service. They even had the occasional squad come in from other countries to train with the US troops.

Captain Anthony Sullivan, known to his friends as Tony, stood in front of a small group of local women whom he'd been teaching to use a computer, as well as how to budget for their household. With the war, so many women had been left to fend for their families while their men were either fighting, or dead. Some of the women he'd taught were married to the very men he was fighting against. But these women didn't get much choice when it came to who they married.

In Iraq, women were treated more like chattel to buy and sell than what they really were: wives, mothers, daughters, and sisters. Tony worried about the women left behind, and with the permission of his commander, he had begun teaching the local women how to financially care for their families. And if he got in a lesson or two about God, and his love of all human beings, then so much the better.

For a fee, the local internet café had agreed to let him use their computers to train the women. It seemed American money went a long way in Kurdistan.

Tony never turned his back to the front door. He kept an eagle eye out for trouble, as did the internet café owner, who liked the Americans. So when Tony heard some yelling outside the café, where he always had two guards stationed, he knew trouble was brewing.

The women ignored the shouts; it was a regular occurrence in their part of the world. Half the time, the shouts were just two people haggling over some deal or other. But Tony knew the difference, especially when his radio squawked a code word—*Rain*.

"Alright, let's get to the back of the building." Tony knew the back had an emergency exit, but it was most likely blocked by the recent shipment Kalid had received. Cursing under his breath, Tony tried to get all the women to safety before the fighting began.

The women, for their part, did quite well. They were chatting in their own local dialect, so he didn't understand them, but he could tell from the way their eyes squinted they weren't afraid, just frustrated. The local Kurdish women rarely wore the black head coverings, or hajib, that covered most of their faces. Kurdish women let their faces be seen. The one thing Tony appreciated the most about the Kurdish culture: they didn't want to hide their women behind black. Instead, the women chose to wear colorful, long flowing dresses that made them look beautiful and feminine, not like they were wearing black potato sacks.

Sounds of gunfire whistled through the air and Tony knew they were in the middle of trouble. He placed himself between the women and the front door. "Quick, get these boxes out of the way." He pointed to the pile of boxes and crates that covered part of the back door, and the interpreter translated for him.

The front door burst open, and a man wearing all black and a vest laden with plastic explosives, probably stolen from a US base, began yelling in Arabic. He obviously wasn't Kurdish, and he most likely wasn't even from this part of Iraq. Unfortunately, none of that mattered at the moment. All that mattered was getting everyone out of the café before the suicide bomber made good on his threat to blow them all to hell.

It was amazing what went through Tony's mind as he realized he wasn't going to leave here alive. Thoughts of his family back home quickly came and went. Instead of focusing on what he was about to lose, he focused on the One who could help those that would live. He prayed the women would survive and the men and women in his squad outside would be alright.

Tony faced the man blocking the entrance and put his hands up. In his best Arabic, he said, "Please, don't hurt the women. They only wanted to learn how to manage their household finances while their husbands were away. They did nothing wrong."

Several ideas quickly entered his mind on ways to talk the bomber down, but when he looked into the eyes of the man whose hand was on a kill switch, he knew there was nothing to say. The anger and steely determination glaring back at him sent shivers down his spine.

"Allahu akbar!" the man screamed as he moved his thumb off the switch.

Tony twisted to the right and tried to get behind the overturned table, but he was too late. The last thing Tony saw was a bright light, and he prayed God would be waiting for him on the other side.

Chapter 1

"Hope, we can't thank you enough for agreeing to come and help us out." Annie Baker pulled her niece in for a hug. "This means the world to us."

"Can't…breathe…" Hope feigned as she returned her aunt's hug. It wasn't that the hug was too tight, it was that she felt awkward with all the gratitude. Truth be told, she was the one who should be grateful. If she had to stay home one more week, she was going to commit hari-kari, or something worse—like take her ex back.

Annie pulled back and smiled from ear to ear. "Oh, sweetheart." She pinched Hope's cheek and sighed. "It's going to be nice having another woman around. Your Uncle Jesse and the two ranch hands we have aren't the same as having a woman to talk with."

Heat made its way up Hope's neck and into her cheeks. She couldn't believe all of the fuss about her coming to help her aunt and uncle on their farm. The moment her cousin Dana had come home from her honeymoon, Hope had called and asked to come visit. Hope and Dana had been very close, until this past year. They had spent summers visiting each other and kept in touch all year long.

While Hope had been at the wedding, she was only there as a guest, and didn't get to see much of her cousin. And when she watched Dana walk down the aisle, Hope realized how much she had missed out on while she had been under the spell of that scoundrel.

The only reason Hope wasn't a bridesmaid was because she had been too wrapped up in an unhealthy relationship. When it finally went sideways, and Hope reached out to her cousin, Dana had already picked out her bridesmaids. Hope really regretted ignoring her cousin all those months. But she knew if Dana had heard her voice, she'd know exactly what Hope had been up to, hence the radio silence on her part. The last thing she wanted was her cousin finding out what she'd been doing.

So, when Aunt Annie invited her to come and help at their farm, she jumped at the chance to renew her closeness with her cousin, who was really more like her sister. Hope had been at the Baker Farm for only three days, but she'd seen Dana twice already. And they had plans to go out to dinner tonight, just the two of them.

"Really, Aunt Annie. I'm so glad to be here. You know how much I love you and Uncle Jesse. And this ranch." A sense of belonging hit Hope right in the chest, and she knew she'd made the right choice. It wasn't that there was anything wrong with her family or their ranch, she just needed a change. And this was the perfect place to get her head screwed back on straight. And her heart right.

"Remember that one summer when you were here? I think you and Dana were about twelve. You two had a running bet all summer long on who'd win the most races." Annie leaned back and looked off into the distance, remembering when the girls were younger, and a smile inched across her lips. "Those were the best summers."

"I agree. I always loved coming here and having Dana over to my ranch." Hope giggled when a distant memory came back.

"What's so funny?" A line Hope couldn't remember seeing on her aunt's forehead stood out prominently before her brows moved together in confusion.

Hope rubbed her nose, trying to hide her grin. "Oh, nothing." It was something, but she didn't want to rat out her cousin.

Annie put her hands on her hips and pursed her lips. "Out with it."

Hope never could defy her aunt when she gave her *that* look. Hope felt the disappointment in her aunt's glare, and the last thing she wanted was for her aunt to be upset with her. Even as a kid, she'd never wanted her aunt to be mad at her. Now her mother… Well, that was another story. But Aunt Annie was the adult she had always looked up to and confided in growing up.

With a sigh, Hope quirked her lips to the side and nodded. "Well, I guess it won't hurt now. Dana is married and not living here anymore." Hope looked around and lowered her voice, as though she was about to convey a state secret. "When Dana came to see me one summer, we were thirteen and just starting to like boys." She stopped and covered her mouth, trying to stifle a giggle.

"Oh, please don't tell me that my Dana was caught kissing a ranch hand." Annie looked to the sky and shook her head, almost regretting what was to come.

"Not quite." The boy she had caught her cousin with wasn't exactly a ranch hand. "James was the son of the ranch foreman. And I walked in on them making out in the hay loft." Hope giggled with the memory. James had turned out to be pretty wild. She should have known he would be. The rest of the summer, he'd been caught with two other girls around town, and the boy wasn't even old enough to drive yet. But he did have that cowboy swagger down pat.

Annie laughed, the kind that drew a snort and caused her cheeks to turn pink with embarrassment. "Oh, my. Please tell me James and you never went out?"

Hope waved a hand before her face. "Please, James turned out to be the town player before he even graduated high school." She grinned. "And besides, Dana and I had a motto: sisters before misters. We always stuck to that. If she liked a boy, I never even gave him a second look, even after she left. And if I liked one, she would always investigate him." Hope wished Dana had been there when she had met her ex. Things would have been so much better if she'd never fallen under *his* spell.

"Sooo…" Annie looked at her niece out of the corner of her eye. "Did you leave anyone special back home?"

Hope snorted. "Goodness, no." She shook her head. "I've sworn off men. I need to focus on helping you and Uncle Jesse get back on track since Dana left you high and dry for a *man*." She shivered, knowing good and well that Dana did whatever she could to help her parents in addition to working at the local coffee shop *and* helping her new husband at his own ranch.

Annie sniffed and pretended to swipe a tear from under eye. "I don't know what we would have done without you, dear." But she couldn't hold the charade up for long and a smile crept up her lips before she started laughing outright.

"It feels like I'm home, you know?" Little lines indented between Hope's brows, and she pursed her lips. "I know I have a home with my parents, but this place, this town, has always felt special." She shrugged and shook her head. "I don't know if I'm saying it right, but I love his place as though it was my own home."

Annie pulled her niece in for another hug. "Dear, this is your home. And it always will be. Our door is open to you no matter what. And we've never changed your room." She pulled back and a sly smile began. "Now, Dana's room. That's a different story."

Both laughed thinking about how Annie had already begun making changes to Dana's childhood room. Since Dana had married and moved to the Crooked Arrow Ranch with her new husband, Jerod, Annie had plans to turn the space into her own personal sewing room.

"Do you think I can take a corner and set up my crafts?" Hope grinned, knowing full well that she rarely had time to craft. Most of her free time was spent on horseback. In fact, she looked down at her watch and winced when she realized how late it was. She had a date.

<h1 style="text-align:center">Chapter 2</h1>

"**B**last it all!" Anthony Sullivan, Tony to his friends, was sick and tired of the scratching. He knew it meant his skin was healing, which was a good thing. But when would the scratching stop?

"Tony? Are you alright?" Dana turned from the dough she was kneading and took two steps toward their newest arrival before she realized her hands were covered in a gooey flour. She turned and picked up a dish towel to clean the mess off her hands before she started dripping it all over the floor she had just cleaned.

He didn't seem to hear her question, and his hand went up over the bandage covering his left ear. Or at least, what was left of it. When he felt a hand on his left shoulder, he jumped and released a string of curses any sailor would be proud of. "What?"

Dana jumped back, her heart pounding. "I'm sorry. I didn't mean to startle you. I just wanted to know if you were alright?"

Tony sighed. It wasn't the first time he'd scared the poor woman. He'd also gone off on a few of the men, too. Since losing all hearing in his left ear, he still hadn't grown accustomed to anyone coming up on his left. Especially when they touched him. "I'm sorry." He waved his hands in front of him and grimaced. "I hope I didn't scare you too much."

Dana Stevens was a sweet woman who had recently married Jerod, the owner of the Crooked Arrow Ranch, who helped wounded veterans heal and reacclimate to society. One of the other vets had likened it to a halfway house for convicts when they were released to the "free world."

He wasn't really sure why he'd been sent to the Crooked Arrow. Tony had prospects for a job when he was finally healed. His hearing would never be right, but with at least one more skin graft, he'd look almost normal. Especially if he wore a hat. It wasn't like he had PTSD so bad he couldn't work. Sure, loud noised bothered him, but he'd be mostly working indoors at his uncle's business. Tony had an MBA, and his uncle had always promised him a spot when he left the army.

Although, since his injury, his uncle hadn't reiterated the offer. But surely he would once the healing was complete, right? It was the family business, after all. Well, his uncle's family business. His parents ran a small ranch in Texas. Uncle Max wouldn't exclude him just because of his ear. Would he?

He'd have to think about that later. Right now, he needed to help Dana know he wouldn't have hurt her. Shoot, he hated killing spiders, there was no way he would hurt a woman as sweet as Dana.

"Tony, I'm sorry. I just forgot about your hearing, that's all. I'll remember next time to approach you on your right side." Dana fidgeted with the dish towel in her hands and bit her lower lip. She looked as though she had more to say, but was doing everything she could to keep her mouth shut.

He sighed. "It's fine. Don't worry. And again, I'm sorry. Sometimes, well…" He sighed and shook his head for the umpteenth time. "I'm still learning that I have to do things differently, that's all."

She nodded and sucked her lips in between her teeth. "Have you…" She trailed off and waved the towel.

"What? Have I what?" Tony tilted his head to the side and looked at her lips. Sometimes it helped to see a person speak. While he wasn't a lip reader, he could get a better understanding of what was being said when he looked at a person's lips and angled his right ear closer to the speaker.

Dana quirked her lips from side to side before speaking. "Have you spoken to Megan about getting a service dog?"

He jerked back, and his eyes widened. Why in the world would Tony Sullivan need a service dog? It wasn't like he suffered from PTSD, much. And he still had all of his limbs, and both eyes worked fine now. At first, the left eye was a bit fuzzy, but the swelling had gone down, and his vision was back to normal. His only real issue was the lack of hearing in what remained of his left ear. That didn't require assistance from a dog.

"I'm sorry, Tony. I didn't mean to offend. But"—she bit her lip—"I'm no doctor and I haven't worked with service dogs, but have you seen how Rogue helps steer Sam away from danger? I just wondered if a service dog could help you somehow? Maybe warn you when someone was coming up on your left?" Dana shrugged in an attempt to downplay the situation.

She was just trying to help, but it still rankled him to hear her say he couldn't do something on his own. He knew there was an issue, but it wasn't a permanent one. Well, okay, so maybe his hearing loss was permanent, but he'd adapt. He would learn to anticipate when someone was on his left. He didn't need hearing for that. His eyes were in great shape and so were his other senses. In fact, he'd learned recently that when someone lost one sense, another one would take up the slack. He just had to be patient while his senses worked to compensate for what he'd lost. That was all.

The itching began again in earnest, and Tony's hand instinctively went to the bandage to try and scratch the blasted tingling away. Instead, he hit the plastic tape holding it all together and rolled his eyes heavenward. "I don't think I need a service dog. I'm fine. But thank you for your thoughtfulness." He wasn't sure what else to say.

There was no way he would intentionally try to hurt the woman's feelings. Tony knew she only wanted to help. But he didn't need her help. In fact, he had considered calling up his uncle and asking if he could come home and recuperate there instead. It would be a lot of work for the family, and none of them were good with sickness or injury.

Getting back into the swing of things would probably be the best thing for him. No one in his family would need to help him with his bandages or anything like that. And he didn't have too many doctor's appointments. Although, after the skin graft, he probably would need to have someone drive him back and forth between the VA facility and the house for a few weeks. For some strange reason, he wasn't allowed to drive for at least six weeks after surgery.

Maybe the VA could send a ride for him if no one in his family could take time off from work to drive him? He'd have to call his uncle later tonight to see if it was even possible.

The veterans here at the ranch were so much worse off than he was; of course Dana would think he needed more help than he did. And, if he left, then a spot would open up for someone else who truly needed their help.

Later that night after he hung up with his uncle, Tony couldn't speak. It took him several minutes to even set his cell phone back down on the little secretary in his room. His uncle had denied his request to come home, and what was worse, he'd even said there wasn't a place for him in the family business. A business he was supposed to take over one day. How could that be?

Was his uncle so frightened of how he looked the last time he'd visited? Sure, that was when Tony was still in the hospital recovering. It was before the most recent skin graft. Now that he thought about it, no one from his family had come to visit him again after that. They all had work to do, and since Tony was healing so well, they said it wasn't necessary.

His mom and sister called him weekly, and most of the time he even spoke to his dad for a few minutes. But he'd only spoken to his uncle when Tony initiated the contact. It wasn't like he was a beast or anything. Sure, he didn't like to look at his own scars in the mirror, but they'd go away for the most part, once his recovery was complete. There would be ways to cover up the worst of it. And he didn't need his hearing in his left ear to work at a desk job in a financial consulting company. He'd spend most of his days either on the phone or staring at spreadsheets on a computer.

There would be occasional meetings with clients, but again, he could cover up most of the scarring. But, he realized, he wouldn't be able to cover up the fact that most of his ear had been blown off in that bombing. If only that psychotic suicide bomber hadn't come into the internet café. All he did was teach the women how to use a computer and take care of their household finances. Surely the local men would be happy to have their wives be more fiscally wise, wouldn't they?

Although, the bomber wasn't from Kurdistan, he was actually from Iran. The young man had yelled out a few choice words before flicking the switch in his hand, and that was the last thing Tony remembered.

When he woke up several days later in a German hospital, he'd been surprised not only because he was still alive, but because his main injury was just his left ear: much of it was missing, and he would most likely have permanent hearing loss.

At first, he'd wished he hadn't survived, but once he was stateside and had seen his mother, he was glad he had come home. He'd never admit it to anyone, but it was his mother who gave him the will to keep going and get better as quickly as possible. No way was he going to be the cause of her hysterical crying again.

Tony knew he looked more like the Phantom of the Opera than a US Army officer, but with medical advancements these days, he could get most of his looks back. He wasn't going to grace the cover of GQ or anything like that, but maybe he could get inside Army Times, without a photo, and tell his story of survival and recovery.

What about his plans for his future career? Now he really needed to ensure he fully recovered. He'd show his uncle that he was just as good now as he was before, maybe even better.

And who knows? Maybe Tony would even find a wife to settle down with and have kids. Oh, who was he kidding? Even if he had a decent skin graft, no woman would want a man missing the side of his face. No, women were out. But that was just fine with him; he had way too much to do anyway. He needed to focus on healing, and proving to his uncle that he could work in the financial sector with no issues whatsoever.

So, the next morning when he over overheard Jerod discussing the finances of the ranch with Megan, the counselor, a plan began to form in his mind how he would go about proving his worth.

Chapter 3

Hope's date was with the one creature who never wanted too much from her. Well, okay, so maybe there were times when Juniper demanded too many apples, but what horse didn't want a juicy, sweet treat all the time?

After a long ride around her aunt and uncle's property, Hope was glad to see their barn in the distance. She was hungry and thirsty. That morning, she hadn't planned to be out long, but what she saw had her worried for her family. The plan had been to take a quick ride and come back for breakfast. However, it was closer to lunchtime and her stomach was gurgling just as much as her mind was swirling with the realities of the Baker Farm.

It was the beginning of summer, and it seemed as though the heat and sun was here to stay for quite some time. Hope couldn't remember the last time they'd seen a good rain cloud, let alone a sprinkle. The creek that usually ran through the farmlands and kept their crops watered had already dried up for the season, at least four weeks too soon.

If their land and crops didn't get more water soon, they'd have to petition the water board for more access to the groundwater. And she knew all too well that never went over well. Most likely, her aunt and uncle would lose most of their crops. She would have to take inventory with her uncle and then decide which crops to continue watering and which ones to let dry up. They still needed their well water for drinking, cooking, bathing, cleaning, and watering their animals.

Thankfully, the Baker Farm didn't have a lot of cattle to water. They basically raised what they needed to feed the family, plus a little extra for bartering. The way they made their money was selling their crops. Sadly, it didn't look like they were going to do very well with the summer and fall markets if it didn't rain soon.

Hope reined in her horse, Juniper, when she was in front of the barn. The dapple mare was only fourteen hands high, but that worked well for Hope, who barely clocked in at five feet four inches. And that was when she was in her boots. Once Hope was back on the ground, she took a handkerchief out of her pocket and wiped the sweat from her face.

Normally, Hope hated wearing hats. She said she didn't look right with hat head, so she rarely wore a hat when she went riding. Although, had she realized how long she would have been out riding, she would have worn one that day. Her red-and-black checked elastic headband that she usually wore across her forehead was almost always enough to catch any drips of sweat coming from her hairline. But today, she needed much more than the soft, flimsy material to catch the water that had dripped down her face.

Hope knew she'd have to deal with a harsh sunburn as well, if the stinging she felt on her cheeks was any indication. Her daily moisturizer had an SPF of twenty, but that wasn't enough for riding in the harsh Montana summer sun for hours at a time. From here on out, she'd have to remember to put a tube of sunscreen in her tack as well as a baseball cap.

While Hope had grown up on ranches and farms her entire life, she had never enjoyed wearing a full-blown cowgirl hat. Even when she'd tried larger sizes, the tightness always gave her a headache. Her brothers always teased her saying she had a big head. She didn't, she just had a sensitive head. Hope didn't even like wearing a ponytail. Any pressure on her scalp hurt for some strange reason.

As she drew her dirty handkerchief across her face again, she noticed her uncle striding toward her.

"So, what did you see?" Uncle Jesse stopped in front her, and his tall frame helped to block most of the sunlight from hitting her directly in the eyes.

Not wanting to be outside even one more minute, she walked around him and headed for the back door of the farmhouse. "Let's go inside. I'm hot and thirsty."

"And I'll bet hungry, to boot. Your aunt was worried when you didn't show up for breakfast today." Jesse reached around her and opened the back door that led into the mudroom. "I told her you must have been too engrossed in taking a look at the entire farm to realize the time."

Hope chuckled. "You know me too well." Her stomach gurgled its approval for talk about food. The sweet scent of maple-wood bacon and the sounds of sizzling caught her attention, and all thoughts about the state of the farm fled in favor of what she was about to eat—her aunt's famous BLTA sandwiches. She licked her lips and prayed her aunt also had freshly made potato chips to go with it.

One of the best things about living on a farm was that most food was prepared fresh, just the way she liked it.

Later that evening, after a long, hot shower, Hope was dressed up and ready to have a night on the town with her cousin. Not that they would be out late, farmers and ranchers tended to hit the hay by nine, or sooner. But she was ready to eat out and catch up with her cousin again. She'd been in town for over a week now, and they'd gone out to dinner twice. She was beginning to wonder if Dana liked her husband or not. She seemed eager to hang out with Hope a lot. But then again, she and Dana hadn't seen much of each other for over a year. And she'd only been in town for nine days.

"So, how's it living with a ranch full of testosterone?" Hope giggled as she drove her cousin away from the Crooked Arrow Ranch. She glanced back in her mirror and noticed there were several good-looking and strapping men watching them leave. When she stopped at the edge of the drive, before turning to head into town, she glanced back again.

In her rearview mirror, Hope noticed two men still standing on the porch watching them. One she knew was the young flirt, Skeeter. He seemed harmless enough, but not her type. Skeeter was a bit of a mountain-man. He wore a scruffy beard and had dark hair and dark eyes to match. But there was always a twinkle in those eyes that made her feel safe with him.

Hope had seen a few tattoos on his forearm, and she'd heard a rumor that he rode a motorcycle. Not that there was anything wrong with motorcycles; most farmers and ranchers had dirt bikes and four-wheelers. But she got the impression Skeeter had belonged to a biker gang. Which seemed out of place for a young, wounded veteran. Maybe he had been part of a gang before joining the service?

But the other man, she wasn't sure who he was. However, he wasn't a scruffy mountain-man. No, he was more dangerous than that. The clean-shaven, blond-haired, blue-eyed Adonis was much more likely to cause her a whole world of hurt, if she let him. Maybe that was why Dana hadn't introduced them? Her cousin probably knew that man was the sort to break through any walls or defenses she had set up.

And Hope had plenty of defenses put up, ready to defend against an invasion. But one smoldering look from that man, and well, let's just say it wouldn't take too much for him to scale her walls and break down her fortress.

"Did you hear me?" Dana looked to her cousin with a smirk, then glanced back at the house. "Ah, yes." She nodded and turned forward again. "I think this is going to be one fun summer."

"And what's that supposed to mean?" Hope pursed her lips but kept her eyes on the road in front of her. It wasn't that she was necessarily worried about other vehicles; she was more concerned with the lone cow or steer that always seemed to be meandering down the deserted highways when she was anywhere near a ranch.

"They're both really nice guys, but I think you'd chew up and spit out poor Skeeter before he knew what hit him. So take it easy on that one, alright?" Dana seemed to have a soft spot for the young cowboy.

"What's his story anyway? I hear he's part of a motorcycle gang?" Hope couldn't remember who had said it. Maybe she'd overheard someone talking the other day when she was in town getting coffee at Frenchtown Roasting Company, but she wasn't sure.

A soft chuckle escaped Dana, and she put a hand over her mouth. "Sorry. I don't know where you heard that, but Skeeter's not part of any gang. He's a nice guy, and I think he did at one time have a motorcycle, but a gang? He's too sweet-hearted for that."

Hope nodded and thought for a moment before trying to slyly ask about the one man she really did want to know more about. "And the other one?"

Dana arched a brow and suppressed a smile. "That would be Anthony Sullivan. His friends call him Tony. And he's one to watch out for."

"Really? Is he part of a gang?" A dangerous vibe definitely came off the man, but not that sort of dangerous. Hope felt as though Tony would yank her heart out and smash it, but not literally. Her classification of him as a heartbreaker was more figurative.

"No, silly." Dana shook her head and giggled. "I mean he's just the sort that would catch your eye. But, he's not ready for a relationship yet."

Hope glanced at her cousin for a moment before turning her attention back to the road. "What does that mean?" While she had only seen his right-side profile, he looked fine to her. Yeah, she noticed the edges of a bandage on his head, but these were wounded vets. There was an expectation of some sort of physical injury.

Although, the longer they sat there in silence, the more Hope wondered if maybe the handsome man was dealing with some pretty serious mental issues. She'd read about PTSD but didn't know anyone who suffered from it. At least, not any military folks. "What brought him to the ranch?"

Dana pursed her lips. "You know I can't talk about a person's medical issues. There are all sorts of laws and regulations. You should have seen the stack of papers I had to sign before I could move on the property after I married Jerod." She shook her hand out, remembering the cramp she'd gotten from signing all those papers. Who did paper anymore? Wasn't everything supposed to be electronic nowadays?

"Sorry, I shouldn't have asked. It's none of my business anyway. And before you ask, I'm on a man-fast for the rest of this year, maybe even longer." While Hope had found him handsome, at least what she'd seen of him, she knew better than to get involved with anyone. If she was going to help her aunt and uncle get their farm back in the black, she needed to put all of her mental, and physical, energy into that, not a man.

"Man-fast?" Dana chuckled. "What in the world is that?"

Hope shrugged while her mouth shut itself tight. She hadn't meant to say those words, or give the impression that there was anything wrong with men, or her. But she knew her cousin well enough to know that even from the little bit she'd said already, Dana would figure it all out soon enough.

"Come, on, Cuz. Time to spill the beans." The pleather seats screeched as Dana moved to get a better look at her cousin. "Tell me all. You know I'll find out one way or another."

And she would, too. Hope didn't doubt it one bit. But how much to share, that was the question. She took a moment to gather her thoughts and then began. "You know I was dating a guy, right?"

Dana didn't say anything, she just nodded.

"Well…" Hope sighed. "He turned out to be a real scoundrel. The sort that will most likely spend a good portion of his life in jail." She winced when she thought back to the first glimpse of his true nature and wished she'd have run then.

"I figured as much." Dana didn't judge her cousin, but she did purse her lips and keep the rest of her thoughts to herself.

"I'm sorry I wasn't around much the past year. But most of all, I'm sorry I didn't return any of your calls to be your bridesmaid. I'll always regret that." A pain shot through Hope's chest, and regret filled her as she shook her head.

A hand covered hers on the steering wheel for just a moment. Then Dana pulled it back. "I know. I really wish I would have come to see you instead of just let it go. That is something I'll always regret."

Hope felt the anguish coming from her cousin and sniffed. She wasn't going to cry, not when they were on their way to a fun night out.

When Dana wiped an errant tear from her cheek, Hope knew a subject change was in order. "So, tell me about married life on the ranch."

Dana grinned and looked to her cousin. "How much time you got?"

With a laugh, the serious emotions fled from both women, and they chatted about life on a ranch and living with a bunch of men.

"You know, most of those guys are only wannabe cowboys." Dana chuckled and bit her lower lip.

Hope figured her cousin was holding back a few good stories and wondered how she could get Dana to share some dirt on those guys. "Aren't most of them from the city originally? Did any of them grow up on a ranch, or a farm?"

Dana nodded. "I'd say most are city slickers. But a couple grew up around ranches and animals and they might know a thing or two. Although, the way they all act sometimes, you'd never know."

"Okay, how about some examples? Until you tell me some of the craziness, I'll have to believe none of them know what they're doing." A tinge of guilt plagued Hope as she knew most of what went on at the ranch was confidential, but surely there were some stories that could be shared.

Or at least, Hope prayed she could get some juicy details. Not that she'd go about sharing any of it, she just wanted to know what she was dealing with. If she went over to visit her cousin at the Crooked Arrow, and she knew she would, then she should at least be a little bit prepared to deal with the not-so-cowboy cowboys.

When Dana arched a brow and looked to Hope, she put her hands up. "Hey, I'm not looking for dirt, just to understand what you're talking about. You don't even have to name anyone. Just tell me a story."

Dana snort laughed. "Really? You want a bedtime story?"

"No, just tell me something in general without naming anyone specific." Hope paused. "Or maybe nothing at all. I don't want you breaking any confidences."

"Hmm. Let me think." Dana thought about some of the shenanigans the men had gotten up to, smiling when one story came to the front of her mind. "Okay, so they guys have been talking about setting up a cow cuddling program. And not just for themselves."

Hope interrupted, "Wait. Cow cuddling? Is that really a thing?" She'd read a romance recently where a ranch introduced cow cuddling, but she'd thought it was just part of the story. Fiction. Not real. Something different for the author to write about.

"Actually, it is. A lot of new studies have come out recently about ways to help the injured and those suffering from mental issues like PTSD. The service dog program is something that we are introducing, but not all veterans will qualify for a dog."

Dana paused, continuing after they passed the entrance to the last ranch on the road into town. "In fact, that ranch we just passed has a small herd of Scottish Highland cows. They have horns, naturally. But when you breed them with

Angus cattle, they don't grow horns. And the best part is that they do have the shaggy, warm coat of the Highland cows, or kews, as the Scottish pronounce it."

"Really?" Hope couldn't fathom the concept of hugging a cow to feel good. "But the cows are so large. I'd rather hug a dog. But that's me."

Dana laughed and shook her head. "The service dogs aren't for cuddling. They actually work to help a person with so many aspects of daily life. But cows, they do seem to like the human interaction."

"Okay, so what about those videos of cows chasing their ranchers and attacking their four-wheelers?" Hope laughed when she thought about the one she had seen recently where the wife was trying to tag the cow, and it wasn't having it. The cow chased her across a field, and when the woman tried to get into her Gator, the cow headbutted it and flipped the machine, with the woman in it. She was fine, but the Gator's door was smashed.

Dana grinned. "I love those videos. But each cow breed has different temperaments. The Angus and the Highland cows are both pretty docile creatures. And when they breed, the horns are gone and you get a great cow for cuddling."

"How do you know about this?" Hope arched a brow and stole a glance next to her. She noted Dana's cheeks had turned pink and she was staring straight out the front window.

"Well, that might be one of the funny stories." Dana shrugged but said no more.

"Please don't tell me that those guys tried hugging a bull? Or one of those crazy cows you mentioned?" The thought brought giggles to Hope, and she really hoped there was video, or at least a photo, of the event.

As they approached the town, both ladies quieted down, but Hope kept running a loop through her brain of what those wannabe cowboys may have been up to with the cows on the Crooked Arrow Ranch. She knew there was one guy who milked a few dairy cows every day. She'd even tried his cheese, and it was pretty good. But she just couldn't imagine that guy, Mark? Or was it Matthew? "Hey, what's the name of that guy who's quiet and spends most of his time with the cows?"

"That's Mike Blankenship. And no, he wasn't the one who tried hugging the Jersey cows." A strange sound came from Dana.

When Hope looked over at her, she noticed Dana trying hard to hold in a laugh. Her lips were sucked in, and her face was turning red.

"Whoa, now. There's a story there. Come on, tell me." Hope prodded, and eventually Dana gave in.

"Alright, but you have to keep this to yourself."

"I promise, I won't gossip. Just tell me. Was it Jerod who tried to hug a cow?" If he was the culprit, then Hope was going to find a great way to razz him without letting on how she found out. And she was going to see if there were pictures.

Laughing, Dana shook her head. "No way. He knows better. It was Skeeter, but mind you, the others dared him."

"Wait, Skeeter tried to hug a Jersey cow?" The thought of that guy wrapping his arms around a miking cow didn't sound very funny. Well, anyone hugging a cow could be funny, but Skeeter? "What happened?"

"Well, for starters, it wasn't a cow." Dana pursed her lips and stared at Hope until it dawned on her.

Hope put a hand to her mouth and about exploded with laughter. "Oh, my. He didn't?"

"He did. Well, he tried, but wasn't very successful. I'm just glad he survived it and didn't get hurt." Dana shook her head and chuckled.

"Why would he accept a dare to hug a Jersey bull?" Hope turned her head when they came to a stop. "It was a Jersey bull, right?"

Dana nodded. "It started as a stupid dare. Skeeter wasn't going for it, but when Arthur and Dixon started calling him chicken, well. You know men."

"Don't you mean boys?" Hope whistled and wished she'd been there for that one. "Doesn't Skeeter have an issue with his legs? How'd he get away without injury?"

"That's where it got good. The guys felt so bad that Skeeter actually went out into the bull pen, they knew they had to do something when ol' Custard began snorting and pounding his hoof in the ground."

Hope interrupted, "Sounds like something you'd see in Spain with the running of the bulls."

"Something like that. Anyway, Mike of all people ran out with a red horse blanket and started yelling to get Custard's attention. He even waved the blanket like a cape." Dana laughed and sighed. "Oh, I wish I'd gotten it on video. It was classic. Something you might have seen on *Laurel and Hardy*, or one of those old black-and-white classic shows."

Hope pounded the steering wheel and howled with laughter. "Oh, this is too good. And no one outside the ranch knows about it?"

Dana shook her head. "Nope. The guys all promised not to say a word. It's been over two months and so far, no gossip, so I have to believe they kept their word."

"Wow, I never would have guessed. Men seem to be worse at keeping secrets than women. Especially when the secret is so juicy." Hope wondered if it was because they felt so bad about tricking Skeeter into getting near the ornery bull. The Jersey bulls were some of the meanest ones out there, truly aggressive. "But no one was hurt, right?" Hope would have felt rotten if anyone had been hurt and she was laughing over it. But since Dana was laughing, she guessed all was fine.

"Only pride. Thankfully, Mike got out of there in time with his bullfighting stunt. And he stayed far enough away that he was also able to run and jump the fence by the time Custard got close to him." The amount of information Dana had was more than Hope could have wanted.

"How many cowboys does it take to distract a bull?" Hope started out with a joke, but couldn't finish it.

"Too many to count." Dana finished for her.

Over dinner they joked and shared stories, but Dana stayed away from all discussions about Hope's ex-boyfriend, which Hope was grateful for. The last place she wanted to discuss Billy was in public. She knew enough about small towns to know the second anyone overheard something juicy, it would be all over town faster than stink on a skunk. And the story would be stinkier, too.

"Okay, so what's going on with all of these signs about a Fourth of July Parade?" Over the past week, Hope couldn't go anywhere without seeing signs, banners, and hearing people talk about the upcoming parade.

Dana bounced in her seat and oozed excitement. "Oh, this is the best part. Do you remember when we were kids and the floats would go down Main Street?"

Hope thought for a moment. It had been more than a decade since she'd been in town for the Fourth of July. But images of candy being thrown at them and the taste of snow cones broke through the fog, and she grinned. "I had completely forgotten. Those were some seriously fun times." She tilted her head. "The town still does the parade? Do they have the snow cones, too?" Not that she was big on the frozen treat since she'd grown up, but there was something to be said about nostalgia.

"Yup, and the ranch has entered with a float."

Chapter 4

"**A**re you sure we're doing this right?" Tony stood back and tilted his head from side to side, gazing at the flowers they'd just put into the large buckets along the rim of the float. "I've seen the Tournament of Roses Parade, in person, and let me tell you, this float looks nothing like those."

Skeeter stood up and scoffed, standing on Tony's right side. "Of course not, we just started. But give it time, we'll get this car hauler looking like a pretty right float." He winked at the roses and nodded. They had used a flatbed car hauler as the base for their float, and a tractor would pull it during the parade.

Tony narrowed his eyes and gawked at Skeeter. "Did you just wink at the flowers?"

With a snort, Skeeter nodded his head. "Yeah, so what? They're pretty nice looking, don't you think? And the women… Boy howdy! They just love roses." With a grin, he leaned over and plucked one perfectly formed rose from the bucket and sniffed it.

"You are one weird dude. You know that, right?" With Skeeter still on Tony's right side, the older veteran turned and picked up more flowers from the wooden crates the florist had delivered. "How is it that the ranch can afford these flowers? I thought they were just barely making it?"

"Where'd you hear that?" Skeeter dropped the rose back in its bucket and turned to glare at Tony. "The ranch is doing just fine. They get money from the VA and other government grants." Skeeter knew his time at the ranch was coming to a close, but he didn't like the idea of the ranch not being there for others like him and his new friends.

With hands in the air, as though he was surrendering to the enemy, Tony backed up a few steps. "Hey, now. I heard a conversation I probably shouldn't have. It sounded like Jerod was complaining that they didn't have enough funds to get by the rest of the year."

"No, no, no. Don't you dare put that out there. Keep your negativity to yourself." Skeeter shook his head violently and paced the ground next to the float. "The ranch can't fold. Too many men like us need places like the Crooked Arrow. I wasn't going to heal up nearly as well in a VA rehab center where most go to die. I needed a place like the Crooked Arrow, so I could find myself, and my future." He sat down and ran his hand through his unruly dark hair.

Now it was Tony's turn to become upset. He didn't think the ranch was on the verge of closing, just that they needed to make a few changes. But he'd already caused Skeeter to go into a tailspin. Tony knew from experience that the best way to get Skeeter back to his normal, annoying self was to get him to think about something positive. And in that young man's case, that something was a pretty girl.

"Say, why don't we go over and get a root beer? I heard the tavern has a new girl working and she's very pretty." Tony grinned when Skeeter's head popped up and his crazy eyes began to clear.

"Did you say pretty new girl?" A slow smile crept across the young man's face, and Tony knew he had him.

"Come on, my treat." Tony picked up his Stetson, its felt the same dark brown of the Tecovas he wore.

Before exiting the barn, he checked that his hat was covering up most of his injury. The last thing he needed was to cause any of the villagers to run away from him screaming, "Monster, monster!" Or worse, running toward him with pitchforks and blazing torches. He shook the thoughts out of his head. Last night the guys had watched some old monster movies on the local cable access channel. He'd have to remind himself to not do that again, especially right before bed.

The reports about a pretty, young thing serving drinks and cleaning tables at the local tavern were mostly true. She was pretty. But young? Tony guessed age was just a number, and young versus old was all about perspective.

"Older woman. I love older, more-experienced women." Skeeter grinned and wiped his face before heading toward the new waitress.

The woman was tall, especially with her three-inch heels. Tony had no clue how a woman could work all day long in shoes that high; they had to hurt. He'd stick with his cowboy boots, thank you very much. She was pretty with her long dirty-blond hair. He wasn't close enough to see the color of her eyes, but when she smiled at the table full of men ordering drinks, her eyes sparkled, and her face shone. She really was beautiful, but he wasn't here to gawk at pretty girls. Nope, he was here to help his buddy feel better.

Tony stayed back and watched, trying not to laugh when the woman barely noticed Skeeter. He tried to get her attention and he even started talking to her, but she walked away without looking back. To be fair, she was busy. There was a crowd of people in the tavern ordering dinner, drinks, and even dessert. They had come right at the beginning of suppertime. And with the summer activities all going strong, it made sense the place would be packed. Especially since the tavern and diner were the only two places in town to get a sit-down dinner. Unless you counted the local Gas 'N' Go and their picnic tables out front, which Tony didn't.

In fact, the tavern held so many diners already that the only places to sit were now at the bar. Skeeter had chosen the empty spot at the end of the counter. When he was done waiting for the waitress to look his way, and she didn't, he looked to where Tony stood grinning.

Tony decided to give the poor fella a break, and he headed over to join his friend for a root beer. Maybe he'd even order fish-and-chips. Dinner was included at the ranch, but sometimes it was nice eating out. And the vibe in this place was high-energy, unlike most dinners at the ranch.

Well, that wasn't true. It was high-energy at the Crooked Arrow Ranch dinner table, but it wasn't always fun. Not like in the tavern where old friends and new sat and shared drinks and dinner. He overheard several snippets of conversation and realized some of these people were going to stay all the way through the Fourth of July parade.

In addition to the flower show at the Big Sky Christmas Tree Farm, there was also a rodeo coming up this weekend not too far away in Missoula. And they had some good fishing streams all within an hour's drive from town. There was plenty for tourists to do. And when the construction on the new bed-and-breakfast in town was completed, there'd probably be even more tourists.

Tony wasn't sure how he felt about all of the extra people walking about town. But he did know it was good for the local businesses, and he figured that would be good for the ranch as well. Especially if he could talk Jerod into doing a few new things that would be tailored to tourists, like cow cuddling. They'd have to make sure there wasn't another Skeeter incident and keep the bulls away from the barn. Docile and sociable cows only. Just the thought of anyone trying to get near Custard again not only brought a smile to his face, but caused his body to involuntarily cringe at the memory.

Poor Skeeter. He was always the butt of the jokes and pranks. But the man took it all in stride, and he usually found ingenious ways to get back at the guys. Although, the skunk was a bit too far, in Tony's opinion. Dixon had had to take three different tomato juice baths before Dana allowed him back in the house. Then it was another week before anyone would sit down to a meal with him. He'd had to take his meals outside on the patio. One night, they'd even told him to scat to the yard so they could barbeque, because nothing made good meat tougher to eat than the stink of skunk still lingering in the air.

"So, you ask her out yet? Or does the Skeeter style take more time?" Tony chuckled when he sat down next to the ranch's biggest flirt.

"Nah, she's not my type." Skeeter looked at the bartender and attempted to get his attention.

Once the man came over, they both ordered root beer and fish-and-chips. And Skeeter's demeanor, while better than before, wasn't as good as when he'd first seen the pretty waitress.

"Skeeter, I think you might want to forgo women for a while. Maybe try a fast. We don't need women mucking up our lives." Tony had already planned on doing a fast, it was just going to take him through the rest of his life. But the young man next to him only needed to take a short break. Tony knew for a fact that the guy had recently been out with two different women in one week. Thankfully, they were both tourists and had left town already.

"Maybe I'll go apply for a job at the new bed-and-breakfast when it opens. I can meet a lot of pretty girls as they come to town." Skeeter's eyes widened, his grin stretching from ear to ear.

Tony sucked in a breath at the same time he tried eating a fry. He coughed and pounded on his chest, trying to dislodge the piece of fried potato stuck in his esophagus.

"Are you sure your husband is alright with you leaving him so much lately?" Hope took a sip of her sweet tea and worried that something might be wrong with Dana's new marriage.

They'd been out three times for dinner, just the two of them, in the past week alone. Not that Hope was complaining. She loved hanging out with her cousin, but the woman was a newlywed. Wasn't she supposed to be tied to her husband's hip for the first year or so? It had barely been a month since they'd married.

Dana took a bite of her fish-and-chips and grinned when she noticed two familiar cowboys inside the local tavern where she and Hope were having dinner. "Don't worry about Jerod, we spend all day long together. When you live and work in the same place as your husband, it's nice to get out with the girls a few times a week. He understands."

Instead of putting a fork of beer-battered cod into her mouth, Hope set the utensil back on her place and took a hard look at her cousin. "Is the honeymoon already over?"

Chuckling, Dana shook her head. "That's not it." She bit her lower lip. "I love Jerod, I really do. But it's an adjustment getting used to living with so many men. I swear, if one more guy farts or burps in my presence and then laughs, I'm going to smack him upside his head." She slumped back in her chair.

Hope laughed. "I wondered what it might be like living with so many men. When do you think you're going to get some female veterans?"

"Not soon enough." Dana looked toward Skeeter and Tony who were now sitting at the bar. "Do you think we should invite Skeeter and Tony to join us? We do have a table for four."

Hope looked over her shoulder and noticed Skeeter slouched in his seat and staring down into his drink. Hope wasn't sure what had the normally happy man down, but she felt bad for him.

Tony had his back toward her so she wasn't sure if that man was also sad, or trying to help Skeeter feel better. But either way, this would be her chance to get to know Tony. They hadn't really met yet; she'd only seen him in profile from a distance several times. "Sure, why not."

After Dana came back to the table with both men, Hope did a double take. She tried very hard not to stare at the man, but he was nothing like what she had expected. Her heart beat hard in her chest, and a tad bit of fear crept up when she saw the scars on the left side of his head.

"Hope, you know Skeeter, right?" Dana glared at Hope and pointed to the cowboy in question.

Hope turned her attention to Skeeter and blinked a few times before she smiled. Guilt needled her over her reaction to Tony. "Yes, I think the entire town knows this guy." Her wooden smile didn't fool Dana, but Skeeter seemed happy to say hi to her.

"Have you met Tony?" Dana asked.

Hope reminded herself that Tony had been injured serving their nation. He didn't need her fearing him, he needed her to act normal and be nice. Before she turned her head, her smile formed, and it felt right, real. Like something she'd give Jerod when seeing him. "Hi, it's so nice to meet you." She gave him a little wave when she noticed his cool demeanor.

Most likely, Tony had sensed her initial reaction to him, and he wasn't happy. She couldn't blame him, though. It was a rude reaction, and she knew it. All she could do now was try to ignore the glaring red streaks and… Well, she didn't need to think about what the side of his head looked like. What she needed to do was look him in the eye without any fear or pity.

While Hope may not be experienced with injured veterans, one thing she knew about men in general: They *hated* pity. Especially when it came from women they didn't even know.

Tony didn't really reply, instead he grunted and looked down at the seat.

"Well." Dana took her seat.

Both men sat down once the ladies were seated. The tension was so thick one would have a tough time cutting it with a giant chef's knife.

It was Skeeter who spoke first. "So, have you seen our float yet?"

Hope looked to Skeeter whose bright eyes and large smile helped her to feel more comfortable, and she relaxed her shoulders once she realized how tense she had become. "No, I heard you were entering one, but Dana hasn't shown it to me yet. How big is it?"

That got everyone laughing.

"Don't get your hopes up, Hope." Dana grinned. "The guys all insisted on doing it themselves. I'm not allowed to even see it until it's all done."

Hope realized everyone at the table seemed to relax the more they continued to banter about the float.

Even though Dana and Hope had their food already, Tony had said they should finish their dinner before it got cold. Just as they ate their last bites, the men's dinners arrived. This time, the pretty waitress looked at Skeeter and smiled.

For the first time, Hope saw Tony grin. She kind of liked it when he smiled. His eyes lit up, and she noticed a little dimple in his chin. It was adorable. She couldn't help but return his smile.

"So, it looks like you finally got the pretty waitress's attention. Whatcha gonna do now?" Tony's teasing remark sent a flurry of butterflies through Hope's stomach.

She prayed her reaction was only because of his sudden changed in demeanor. There was no way Hope Lowry was going to find herself attracted to the tall, blond man with the turquoise eyes that reminded her of Cracker Lake on a sunny day. The fact that he filled out his green-and-black checkered button-up cowboy shirt with strong muscles wasn't going to count.

Tony Sullivan was a good-looking man, even with his scars. But Hope Lowry was done with men. At least for a good long while. She reminded herself that she was in Frenchtown to help her aunt and uncle on their farm, as well as to get over the scoundrel she'd recently broke up with. And Tony didn't deserve to be her rebound guy.

"I'm gonna ask her for her phone number." Skeeter sat up taller in his chair and puffed his chest out, as if he had already scored a date with the pretty woman.

Hope looked from Skeeter to Melody, the waitress, and hoped she'd let him down easily. She knew the waitress was already dating someone else, and they were pretty serious from what she'd seen.

Dana pursed her lips and looked at Skeeter. "You know, you might want to look elsewhere for a date."

"Nah, she's exactly what I need." Skeeter took a bite of his fish after dipping it into the tartar sauce. Then he dipped a couple of fries into the malt vinegar.

Hope bit her lip trying to keep quiet. It was none of her business. But she'd hate to see Skeeter make a fool of himself. She looked across the table to Dana who was trying to stifle a laugh.

When Tony leaned her way and whispered, "What's going on?" she returned the gesture.

"Melody, our waitress," Hope said under her breath, "is already dating someone."

The sparkle in Tony's eyes when he grinned sent shivers down Hope's spine. If he didn't stop smiling, she was going to be in trouble. "Let him figure it out for himself."

Frowning, Hope wanted to ask why when the woman in question came by their table.

"What else can I get you? Maybe a top off of your drinks and some dessert?" Melody looked at Dana and Hope, ignoring both men for the moment.

Dana grinned, and Hope knew she up to something.

"Sure, I'd like another sweet tea. And how's Hank doing? I hear you two have been seen around town together quite a bit lately. Any news to share yet?" She leaned her elbow on the table, placing her chin in the palm of her hand.

Out of the corner of Hope's eye, she noticed Skeeter deflate, and when Tony glared at Dana, she wished she could laugh. Dana had just gotten both men good. It was most likely payback for some prank that had gone awry at Dana's expense instead of theirs.

A huge smile, the likes she hadn't ever seen on the waitress, spread from ear to ear. "Yes." She extended her left hand and flashed a sparkly diamond ring. "He proposed last night."

Both women at the table erupted in squeals of delight.

"Oh, my gosh. That's so beautiful. When's the date?" Dana asked before Hope could get the words out.

Hope pulled Melody's hand toward her to get a better look and sighed. While the diamond wasn't large, it was sparkly and set in an old-fashioned band with silver filigree. The diamond, maybe only about .30 karats, sat in a square bed surrounded by the same intricate filigree pattern. The work made the diamond look bigger than what it really was.

About six months ago, before Hope had realized who she was really dating, she had gone out ring shopping with the expectation that Billy would be proposing soon. Their relationship had gone to the next level, one that she wasn't proud of, and he had said they would get married. Little did she know, he hadn't really planned on asking her to marry him. He had just told her that to get what he wanted, like most men.

But the ring she'd found looked similar to Melody's, except it was a 1.5 karat princess cut with a matching wedding band. It reminded her of something she'd seen in pictures of her great-grandmother. The stones back in those days were much smaller; not many ranchers or farmers could afford such large diamonds. And most women only wore a gold band. But those who were part of the upper crust did tend to wear diamonds, like her great-grandmother had.

When she found her voice, Hope joined the conversation. "Hank has great taste. That ring is exquisite."

"Thank you." Melody pulled her hand back and put it up to her heart. She tilted her head and sighed. "I got lucky with Hank."

"Congratulations," Tony added. Marriage might not be in the cards for him, but he could still celebrate someone else's happiness.

But Skeeter sulked and stayed quiet.

"How about dessert when the men are finished with their dinners?" Dana asked. "They make a wonderful peach cobbler here, serve it up hot and topped with vanilla bean ice cream." She licked her lips in anticipation.

"Oh, that sounds wonderful." Hope sighed and realized she hadn't had a great cobbler in a while. Billy had always made snide comments about her weight and had never wanted her to have dessert. He told her it would add too much fat to her thighs. Even now, when she knew she would never see him again, she almost declined the special treat. But Billy was gone, and no one was going to stop her from indulging except herself.

Hope would never be called skinny. She was short and curvy. No matter how much she worked out, she could never get rid of those last five pounds. And she worked hard. Most farmers and ranchers did. Hope's mom was the same; she always held a few extra pounds, no matter what she did. But her father seemed to like her mom's figure, and her hips. He had said so on many occasions.

Would she ever find a man who liked her just the way she was? No. Stop that train of thought. Hope wasn't going to find a man. She was done with them…for now.

Chapter 5

The next day, after Hope had finished her morning chores, she headed over to the Crooked Arrow to have coffee with Dana and Jerod. Dana had invited her over after dinner the night before. She had said it was to show Hope what life was like on the Crooked Arrow and how disgusting those men were.

Hope smiled when she thought back to the dessert-time conversation. Skeeter and Tony had looked crestfallen when Dana had said living in a house full of men was akin to living in a house full of pigs.

After much debating, Dana invited Hope over to see what the house looked like every morning.

With a spring in her step and a sparkle in her eyes, Hope practically jumped up the front porch steps to the ranch house. Before she even had her fist on the door to knock, Dana opened the door.

"I swear, I wasn't lying last night. Normally, I spend most of the morning picking up their garbage, or remnants of a prank gone wrong." Dana ushered her cousin inside.

Hope stopped at the entrance to the living room. She looked around wide-eyed and silently wondered where the mess was. The room was immaculate. Not a pillow out of place or a piece of trash anywhere. There weren't even coffee mugs sitting on the tables like the last time she'd come to visit. "If this is what you call a disaster zone, sign me up."

Dana put her fists on her hips. "I got up this morning and the entire downstairs was clean. I'd never even been able to get it this clean before."

A chuckle escaped Hope's lips, and she covered her mouth with her hand.

"Don't. You know as well as I do that those two hooligans came home last night and told the rest of the guys what I'd said. I bet they stayed up most of the night cleaning in order to get it looking this good." Dana stepped into the room and sank down on one of the recliners.

"Well," Hope started before she sat down. "At least you didn't have to clean it up today. Maybe I should come over more often?"

Dana smiled. "I doubt they'll do this again. Tony or Skeeter probably dared them to do it."

"Well, I say enjoy it while you can." Hope stood. "So, where's this coffee you were telling me about?"

Dana jumped up smiling and led them both into the kitchen. "Lottie sent me over a new pound of coffee she just roasted the other day. It's strong, but doesn't have a strong coffee flavor. There are notes of cinnamon, chocolate, vanilla, and some spice I can't name."

Hope scrunched up her nose. "Really? That many flavors? Doesn't it come out weird once you brew the coffee?"

"That's the beauty. There's a wonderful bouquet for the nose as well as an exquisite taste for any discerning palate. It's like chocolate tasting. You know, you go to those chocolate factories, and they have several samples out for you to taste. And if you try them all, the flavors mixed together are a perfect pairing."

Hope raised her brows. "Sounds to me like you've become a coffee connoisseur. When did that happen?"

"Really?" Hope turned around and deadpanned. "I've only been working at the Frenchtown Roasting Company for the past five years. Of course I'd learn how to enjoy a good brew."

Hope put up her hands in mock surrender. "Fair enough. Let me try this fantastic cup of coffee for myself."

The two women sat at the kitchen island sipping hot gourmet coffee and eating pieces of the coffee cake Dana had made just that morning.

Hope looked around and over her shoulder conspiratorially. "So, about this float. Do you think we could sneak a peek?"

With a hand over her mouth, Dana suppressed a giggle. "If no one is working on it now, then yes." She bit her lip. "Actually, I do have a couple of cows and a horse I wanted to show you." She winked at her cousin.

"Oh, you know how much I love horses. Let's finish our coffee and head to the barn." Hope winked in return, and the two women downed their coffee before heading out to do some snooping.

"Hi, Sam." Dana leaned down and patted the top of Rogue's head. "Hiya, Rogue. Are you taking good care of your buddy here?"

The dog tilted his head as though he was considering Dana's words then chuffed out his response.

"Oh, he's so cute," Hope gushed. "Can I pet him?"

The normally gruff Army veteran, Sam Marley, rubbed the stubble on his chin and looked to the dog at his side. "What do you think, Rogue? Do you want the ladies to pet you? Or did you want to go inside and get a treat?"

"Hey, now. That's not fair." Dana put fisted hands on her hips and glared at Sam.

Normally, Rogue would have been more interested in treats, but today he wanted to be social. So when he chuffed and rubbed up against Hope's legs, Sam sighed and threw his hands in the air.

"Fine, fine. Be that way, traitor." Sam feigned a glare at his service dog, but there were no hard feelings. Rogue was on a break, his service vest folded and in Sam's hands.

Rogue's tongue lolled to the side, and his back leg shook as Hope scratched the top of his head. He completely ignored his partner.

Service dogs weren't owned in the normal sense. Since they weren't pets, they didn't have the master-pet relationship with their handlers. Instead, a human was given a service dog as a partner. The dog was highly trained, and when in uniform, which was a vest emblazoned with a message stating he was a service dog and not to be touched, he stood by his partner and took good care of him or her.

In the case of Sam and Rogue, Rogue ensured Sam had love and affection and steered him clear of possible mean people. Sam suffered from PTSD and had a prosthetic left arm. Humans could be cruel. Dogs, on the other hand, weren't unless they were trained to be so by cruel humans.

Should a loud sound cause Sam to spiral down into a pit of despair, Rogue was there as an emotional support partner, and he also kept people away while Sam was in a bad state. But one of the best things about Rogue was that he was a fantastic judge of human character. If there was a group of mean men ahead, he'd steer Sam away so he wouldn't catch their attention.

"I love dogs. We have a few back home, and I miss my Missy. But she's also a working dog, so I had to leave her with my parents." Hope leaned down on one knee and gave Rogue a hug. "You're such a good dog, aren't you?"

"Your parents have a service dog?" Sam reached down for Rogue, who came instantly to his side.

Hope shook her head. "No, sorry about that. I meant they work the ranch. Missy helps to corral the cattle and keep wildlife away. She also keeps me company when I'm out riding."

Dana cleared her throat, and Hope got the message. They needed to get inside the barn before the men began working on the float again.

"It was nice meeting you, Rogue. And good seeing you again, Sam." Hope had met Sam before at dinner, but Rogue rarely sat near the dinner table while at the ranch so she hadn't had a chance to meet him yet.

Rogue barked his goodbye and watched as Hope and Dana walked toward the barn as though they weren't sneaking anywhere at all.

Hope thought they should talk like normal and walk into the barn as though they belonged.

But not Dana. "Shh." She put a finger to her lips to silence Hope.

The red barn door was closed, a sure signal they weren't supposed to enter, but Dana pulled it open anyway. She needn't have worried.

"No one home?" Hope asked when she walked inside the barn. It was just as she thought it would be. A tack room was just inside on her right. Stalls of horses were to her left. And a large open area was just past the tack room. A long flatbed trailer stood in the open area.

The parade was only a week away, and this thing looked as though it still needed a good month before it would be presentable. The wooden bed was mostly visible. Along the sides were buckets. Some held flowers, but most didn't. It looked ready to head down to a farmer's market to sell bushels of flowers instead of awing the crowds as a patriotic parade float.

Dana covered her eyes and shook her head. "No, no, no. This isn't going to work at all."

"Do you think Jerod's seen it yet?" Hope slowly walked around the mostly unfinished flatbed trailer.

Dana shrugged. "I have no idea. But I better check. Out of everyone here on the ranch, you and I are the only ones who've seen the parade here."

"Really?" Hope turned her head toward Dana and furrowed her brows. "But, hasn't Jerod been here for like two years already?"

"Yes, but the first year it was all new and he was working on fixing the place up. The second year, he'd only been open for seven months and no one wanted to even attend a Fourth of July celebration." Dana scratched her cheek. "I think they spent their first summer mostly on the ranch trying to figure out how it could all work for everyone."

"Ah, meaning no one wanted to be out in public?" Hope understood that a lot of returning veterans, injured or not, just weren't up for being in the spotlight. And if any of them had attended the Independence Day celebration, they would have been put in the spotlight.

Frenchtown was a small community, and everyone knew everyone else's business. She'd bet the entire region knew exactly who each man was on this ranch and what had brought him here. Even Hope didn't know most of their stories yet, and her aunt's farm was just a stone's throw away.

"Well, we can't let them fail. How are we going to fix this mess?" Dana was too focused on the float to hear anyone coming in.

"What mess? I think it's coming along quite nicely." Dixon leaned against the barn door.

Dana and Hope both jumped.

Hope put her hand on her chest and breathed in a lung full of air. "Don't sneak up on people like that. You're bound to give someone a heart attack."

"Well." Dixon smirked. "If you weren't sneaking in where you didn't belong, you wouldn't have to worry about it, now would you?"

Hope glared at the man and put her hands on her hips. "Now listen here, we belong in the barn."

A deep laughed sounded behind Hope, and she realized what she'd said.

"That didn't come out right. I meant that we have every right to come into the barn and check out the horses." There, that sounded better, didn't it? Hope worried at her bottom lip when she turned around to see who had laughed at her.

"Hope, it's good to see you again." Tony turned to Dana. "I thought Jerod said the barn was off limits until we were done?"

"Hope and I came out here to see if there were any horses we could saddle up and head out for a late morning ride." Dana tilted her head to the side and waited for a response.

It wasn't that Hope thought they were sneaking, snooping, or whatever, but she did feel guilty knowing that they really weren't supposed to be in the barn. Okay, so maybe she did know they were snooping, but she'd never admit it. At least not out loud. She'd stick to the horse story. Yup, she and Dana were planning on riding horses that day. It wouldn't be hard for anyone who knew her to believe.

"Uh-huh. Well." Tony narrowed his eyes. "There are two horses at the front of the barn perfect for you two ladies."

The brows on Hope's eyes raised high, past her bangs and she pursed her lips. "I'll have you know that we're both expert riders." She looked him up and down. "Much better than a wannabe cowboy."

"Ouch." Tony touched his chest. "You might want to learn more about a person before you accuse them of anything."

Hope crossed her arms over her chest. "I could say the same thing to you." She looked down at his boots. They were more decorative then functional. "A real cowboy wouldn't be out in the barn wearing fancy boots designed for a hoedown. He'd be in dirty boots that had seen more mud than a hog."

He smirked. "Really?" Tony looked down at her boots. They were brown ropers that had actually seen better days. His air of superiority left his face when he realized she wore boots that had seen a lot of miles on the trail. Then he put a foot out and looked at his fancy, new Tecovas that still hadn't been worn in yet. Not to mention the turquoise accents that did match several of his shirts were clearly designed for dancing, not mucking stalls or riding horses.

"Exactly." Now it was Hope's turn to smirk. She turned to Dana. "So, how about that ride?"

Dana smiled when she looked between Hope and Tony. "What about the float? I think these guys need our help."

"Oh, no. Please, go out on your ride. Us guys got this." Tony motioned to the horses at the front, knowing full well that those docile mares wouldn't be enough for two experienced horsewomen such as Dana and Hope.

"Come on, I have just the horses for us." Dana chuckled and looked a bit too long at Tony before taking Hope by the hand and leading her to the last two rows where two spirited geldings whinnied their desire to get out and run.

Chapter 6

"Who does she think she is saying I'm a wannabe cowboy?" Tony groused and kicked a clump of dirt at his feet.

Dixon chuckled. "Well, she's got a point." He pointed to the boots that had cost Tony almost four hundred dollars.

"Yeah, yeah. I'm only wearing these now to break them in. I've got plenty of mud-and-dirt-encrusted boots that I wear when doing chores or riding." Ignoring the laughing from his friends, Tony walked over to the tubs of items they were going to use to finish fixing up their float.

He realized that the girls had been right. Not about his boots, in that they didn't know what they were talking about. He had grown up on a ranch, and even though he had planned to work in finance, he still had ranching blood flowing through him. No, the problem was the float. It was a mess.

"I think we may have bitten off more than we can chew with this design." Tony took a couple of steps back and looked hard at the trailer in front of him. There was no way they'd get this done in one week, even with all of them working around the clock.

Dixon walked over to where Tony stood, but he came up on the man's left side.

Even though Tony knew there were other men in the barn, he didn't sense Dixon coming up on his left until it was too late.

Tony struck out with his fist before looking and hit the man in his jaw. He turned his body toward Dixon who stood there with eyes wide and a hand covering his sore jaw. "Oh, sh—" Tony stopped what he had wanted to instinctively say. It was tough being a soldier and not cussing. Instead, he said, "Shitake mushrooms. I'm so sorry. I didn't hear you coming toward me. Instead, I felt a presence and well…" He ran a hand through his hair.

Dixon held up a hand. "No worries, man. I get it. I still jump when a car backfires."

Tony snorted. "I think a lot of people do, even those who never served. That's normal."

"I'm fine. Don't even think about it." Dixon took a few steps back from Tony.

"Ahhh, crackers. I can't even hide out in a barn without causing trouble." The old feeling of inadequacy and shame descended like a storm cloud over Tony's entire being. "I shouldn't even be here." He slapped his thigh and turned to leave.

"Hey, man. Really, this is nothing. I've felt much worse." Dixon grimaced when he tried to smile.

"Gee, thanks. I can't even hit hard when I'm startled. What sort of soldier am I?" He hung his head and ran both hands through his already messy hair. Then he slumped his shoulders and headed toward the tack room. A good, hard ride was what he needed.

"That's not what I meant, and you know it, Captain. From what I hear, you saved the lives of several women in that bombing by your quick actions. Come on, man. Let's go inside and have a coffee." A smile started on Dixon's face before his jaw hurt. "I bet the ladies left some pastry or treats in the kitchen. We could pilfer them."

"I suppose we could." The feeling of inadequacy was starting to wane, and the idea of coffee and something sweet sounded good. "I'm probably getting a bit hangry, so why not."

The rest of the day Tony was in a funk. Nothing seemed to go right for him, and all he could do was growl. At times, he felt more like old Sam Marley than himself. And what was going on with Sam? Tony was perplexed by the major shift in that man's attitude. For the past few weeks, the curmudgeonly ol' guy was *nice*.

Speaking of…

"Hey, Tony. Care to join me on a ride?" Sam greeted Tony with a smile and nod of his head.

Unsure if the guy really was talking to him, Tony looked around and realized he was the only one in the room. Which was odd since the sitting room had had three cowboys sitting in it reading when he'd first entered about an hour ago. Somehow, they had all vanished. It wasn't dinnertime yet. Or was it?

Tony checked his watch and then looked up at Sam who was waiting patiently for his reply. "Uh, sure. I suppose we've got time for a ride." It wasn't like he had anything better to do. Except maybe stew some more over his circumstances. Which wasn't something he normally did.

In fact, Tony had always been the happy go lucky sort. Even back in officer candidacy school, his squad mates had teased him about being happy when they had to hike ten miles with fifty-pound rucksacks on their back. Tony would be dripping with sweat, breathing heavily, and still smiling. His favorite cadence had been – One Mile, no Sweat:

One mile no sweat,
Two miles better yet,
Three miles oh no,
Four miles, gotta go,
Five miles, gotta run,
Six miles, to the sun,
Seven miles feeling good like I should.
In my legs,
In my head,
In my chest,
Feeling good,
Super troop.
Even in the rain.

Now? Now he found himself scowling more and more and smiling less and less. Loud noises were beginning to upset him more. And the nightmares were getting worse. Megan, his counselor, had asked him to attend church services with the group. While he did go, since it was a requirement, he normally sat outside in the foyer and didn't really pay much attention to the sermon.

"Come, let's get you out of your head." Sam waved for Tony to follow him. "I can see you're going to get yourself into a funk if you don't get your mind on something positive."

Tony snorted. "What's positive these days? Other than the fact that I am positively a loser."

"Hey, now. Them's fightin' words." Sam stopped at the back door to the house and grabbed his hat off the peg. "I think you know I'm not the best guy here at being in a good mood, but I've learned a lot over the past few weeks about keeping a positive mental attitude."

"I've noticed." A half smile curved up Tony's face. "But I think a pretty dog trainer has more to do with it than anything else."

Sam looked up at the sky and chuckled when he exited the house. "I'd say God had a lot to do with it, but yeah. The love of a beautiful woman does help smooth out the rough edges."

"Love?" Tony raised his brows and put his hat on his head, following the formerly gruff veteran.

Sam stopped and turned, pointed a finger at Tony, and narrowed his eyes. "Don't you dare say a word to anyone." He looked Tony over. "If I were you, I'd focus on getting right with God. I'm not the only one who's noticed that you don't actually go inside church on Sunday mornings."

"Hey, I hear the sermon. That's all that matters." Tony huffed and walked on to the barn.

"If you say so." Hands in the air in surrender, Sam let the conversation drop. That was, until they were on horseback and out in the back of the property where Tony couldn't easily get away from him.

When Sunday came, Tony thought long and hard about where to sit inside the church. It wasn't that he thought sitting in the foyer was wrong, because it wasn't. Sitting out there alone was easier on his ears, or what was left of them.

For some strange reason, when he sat inside the church with everyone else, the singing hurt his head. Which was odd since he always chose a spot with his left side toward the speakers, so no one would have to see his hideous face. Since he had lost the hearing on his left side, he thought facing his ruined ear toward the speakers wouldn't hurt at all. But it did.

The idea of sitting with his left ear toward anyone didn't sit well with him. Tony was certain that the congregation would stare and point at him as if he was a monster. That was his biggest fear, although he'd never admit it out loud. Shoot, even his own family didn't want to look at or work with him. How would strangers react to the scars?

When he'd first arrived at the Crooked Arrow Ranch, Tony had tried to grow a beard to hide most of his deformity, but he couldn't even do that right. Instead of a full beard, it only grew on the right side and partially on the left, fizzling out at the scar lines. It looked even worse and caused people to notice the missing parts of his head even more.

With all of those memories running around his head, he almost turned tail and ran from the building. But he didn't. If Sam Marley, the surliest veteran he'd ever met could find a way to sit in church and be happy, then Captain Anthony Sullivan could too.

After he took in a couple of deep breaths, Tony slowly inched his way past the second set of doors into the worship center. He stood in the back, on the right side, and looked for a safe place to sit.

The front rows were empty, which was pretty normal for any gathering, church or otherwise. It wouldn't be a bad place to sit if he could keep his head covered, especially the scars. And his partial left ear. While the explosion had taken most of his left ear, there was still a little nib left. The nurse had told him it looked better that way and would help when he was ready to wear sunglasses. But he wasn't so sure.

When Tony noticed where Sam was sitting with his service dog, Rogue, he almost joined them. But they were sitting on the left and in the back, where he knew from experience the sound would cause the worst of the headaches.

No, he knew where he had to sit.

Once he got his courage up, he walked down the right-side aisle, trying to keep out of everyone's way, and took a seat on the front row with his right ear toward the speakers on the side. He left his hat on, knowing that only women were expected to wear a hat in services. Maybe he could get a beanie with those things that hung down over his ears. If that could cover up most of his scars, it might not be too bad.

They had arrived early, and most people were still standing around chatting, so when he noticed someone sitting next to him on his right, he jumped in surprise.

"Jerod?" Tony wasn't sure what the man was doing sitting by him.

"Tony, it's good to see you inside." Jerod looked around before lowering his voice. "Why don't you take my hoodie and put it up over your head instead of the large cowboy hat?"

He knew what Tony was up to and the realization sliced through his heart. Tony wiggled in his seat and turned toward Jerod, pointing the right side of his head toward the rest of the church. "Is it that bad?"

Jerod looked him over and shook his head. "I think that wearing a large cowboy hat in the service will attract more attention than a hoodie will."

"Huh, I hadn't thought about that. Thanks." Tony put the sweatshirt on over his shirt, and once it was on straight, he quickly removed his hat with one hand and pulled the hoodie up over his head with the other, covering more of the scars then he realized was possible.

"If you like, you can sit with Dana and me." Jerod pointed over his shoulder to where Dana sat only a few rows behind him.

The idea wasn't bad, and Tony seriously considered moving with Jerod. That was until he noticed the large speaker hanging on the side of the wall next to their row. "I don't think that's a good idea."

Jerod looked back and before Tony could explain, the man saw the speaker and realization hit him. "Ah, yes. I wondered if the sound was the reason why you didn't sit inside with us each Sunday."

Tony nodded. "That's part of it."

"Alright, how about we move up here to join you? Then you won't be alone."

Hope entered Tony's heart for the first time in days. Maybe he didn't have to be alone on this journey. And maybe his scars didn't scare everyone off. "I'd like that. Thanks."

During the singing portion, Tony caught himself wincing a few times. It wasn't that the singing was bad, or even loud. It was more that there seemed to be a ringing sound in his left ear. Loud noises always seemed to cause him headaches, but this was the first time he'd heard a ringing in his left ear since he'd woke up in that German hospital.

All Tony wanted to do was stick his finger inside his ear and wiggle it. The sensation reminded him of when he was a teenager and had gone to a rock concert and sat too close to the speakers that were larger than his car. For two days after that, he kept wiggling this finger in both his ears trying to clear up the strange sensations that went back and forth between ringing and fog.

But he couldn't. The bandages covered the open portion of his left ear, and they would until after his final reconstructive surgery.

At one point, he put his hand over his left ear, and that helped to ease some of the pain. Maybe there was something that could be done next week to buffer his injured eardrum.

The singing finally ended, and the preacher came up to make the weekly announcements. The rest of the service wouldn't hurt so he took his hand down and listened intently to the man of God. At times, he couldn't hear what he was saying, then at other times, he could hear plain as day. Tony noticed it helped to watch the man's lips as he spoke while keeping his right ear pointed toward the speaker.

When the actual sermon began, Tony was grateful that he'd come. It was a topic he needed to hear more than anything else at that point.

"God cares so much for you that He wants you to give your worries, your burdens, to Him. If you're spending your time worrying about your life, then you aren't trusting in God's Word." The pastor looked around at the congregation who was as silent as the silver screen.

"1 Peter 5:6-8 tells us how to do this. 'Humble yourselves therefor under the mighty hand of God, that He may exalt you in due time, casting all your care upon Him; for He careth for you. Be sober, be vigilant; because your adversary the devil, as a roaring lion, walketh about, seeking whom he may devour.'"

Tony wasn't sure how humbling himself helped give his worries to God, but he was hooked and wanted to know more.

As the pastor went on to explain that by looking to God and letting him take the burdens, a person was acting humbly. There might be some issues that we could deal with on our own, but the large ones?

"Only God can take something so large, such as an illness or injury"—the pastor looked around the congregation, but Tony felt as though he was addressing him directly, even though the man didn't look his way —"and bring healing or the ability to move forward. Remember, God knows how all of our lives will play out, and how they will end. Only He knows the best path for us."

Tony thought about it and wondered if there was something God could have done to stop the suicide bomber. If He knew how it all ended, and what choices people were going to make, why didn't He stop the bomber? While Tony lived, and the four women did as well, the café owner and his son didn't. Why did they have to die and he live?

The first therapist Tony worked with while he was still in the hospital had called it survivor's guilt.

"Captain," the counselor said, "it's normal to wonder why we lived when others didn't. Our brains, and our hearts, want everyone to live. And some of us, especially soldiers, don't think it's fair for innocent people to die while they still live."

Tony remembered his response. "Sir, that bomber was there because of me. And what I was doing to help the local Kurdish women. If I hadn't done that, then the bomber wouldn't have entered the internet café."

The counselor shook his head. "Sadly, that's not necessarily true. People who want to kill themselves in a big way while take others out, like while wearing a suicide vest, will always find a reason to attack innocent people. It wasn't your fault, it was the terrorist's fault. There's a reason we call them terrorists and not something else."

The pastor's loud voice caught Tony's attention, and he came back to the present.

"When you take yourself out of the equation, and recognize that you don't have the power to fix everything, you recognize that God is greater than you are. He is stronger than you are. And only He can do what we can't. Something in our hearts—and souls—click and we stop thinking about why can't *I* do it? And we come to God on our knees and ask Him to take it off our shoulders and ask for His good and perfect will." The pastor smiled and looked around the room, and this time he did look down at Tony and his friends. "That's when God does the impossible, if it's His will. What we have to do is realize that we don't know the entire story."

Tony's head began throbbing, and he wished he'd remembered to bring a bottle of water and some Tylenol. He squirmed in his seat and prayed that God would take the pain away.

"It's like when we read a book," the pastor continued, "sometimes we think we know how the story should go, but then there's a twist we don't see coming. And again, we think we know where it's gonna go from there. But when another twist comes, we sit back in awe and realize that the author just might know best how to weave the details of the story.

"God is the perfect Author. If we let Him tell the story the way He wants, when we get to the end, we'll be so glad that we went on the journey with Him, instead of trying to take things into our hands and make the ending what we want."

A feeling of peace began to take over Tony, and he wondered if God was trying to tell him to sit back and watch as He unfolded His good and perfect story.

The pastor walked across the altar to the other side and looked at a different group of people. "Do you really think you know better than God how our story should unfold? If you were the one to write your story, you'd probably make things go as easy as you could, right?"

The congregation all shook their heads in agreement.

"Think about the people you'd miss meeting along the way. What about those who you might be used to help? Have you ever gone through something difficult, only to learn years later that your experience helped someone come to know God?" The pastor walked back to the middle of the altar and his eyes scanned the room.

"How many of you have heard the story of Jim Elliot? Raise your hands." The pastor looked out and nodded as most of the people raised their hands.

Even Tony knew the story of how five young missionaries to Ecuador were murdered by a tribe of Waodani tribesman. No one could have thought their deaths would be used for glory, but they were.

"I see you all know the name. Did you also know that it was their widows who went back and witnessed to the murderous tribe? An entire tribe of savages who lived by the code of kill or be killed, turned their lives over to God because the wives of the murdered missionaries, and other family members, decided to give it over to God and do as the Lord prompted. Even if it meant they would be murdered as well." The pastor sighed and shook his head. "I don't know if I could have done that."

Tony sat there with tears in his eyes as he recalled the documentary he'd seen and shook his head. Those women had more faith in their pinky fingers than Tony did in his entire body. He didn't think he could go back to Iraq and witness to the terrorists who'd tried to kill him. Of course, the bomber was dead, but his friends might still be alive. Probably still believing in their way of life too.

One thing Tony knew: he had never even considered forgiving the terrorists.

He couldn't.

So what did that say about him and his faith?

But the surviving missionaries had. And so much more.

The pastor went on to challenge everyone to go home and pray and ask God how they could give it all to Him. Ask Him to give them the faith of a mustard seed and then sit back and see how God would lead them to a better life.

"But remember, it might not happen overnight. Sometimes, it takes years. The women didn't go back to the Waodani for five years." The pastor went to his podium and picked up his Bible. "Let me leave you with a quote from James Elliot. He said this while he was still in college, 'He is no fool to give up what he cannot keep to gain that which he cannot lose.'"

Chapter 7

Hope walked out of church that day in a daze. She'd heard about the Elliotts and the Saints and the others who were on that fateful missionary trip. And she was shocked when she heard about Elizabeth Elliott going back to witness to the men who'd killed her husband. But she didn't know many details about the missionaries. All she could think of was finding where she could watch the movie *The End of The Spear* and learn more.

So when she walked past Tony, Dana, and Jerod, she didn't really notice them until Dana called after her.

"Sorry, I was lost in thought." Hope blinked a few times and headed back to where her cousin stood with a growing group of men from the ranch. "That was a powerful sermon, wasn't it?"

Everyone nodded.

"Yeah, have you ever seen that movie?" Dana asked.

"No, I was actually going to go home and see if I could find it online somewhere." While Hope loved talking to her cousin and Jerod, she really didn't want to dawdle. So she pulled out her keys and sunglasses in an effort so show how much she wanted to leave.

"How about you come over and join us for Sunday supper? Jerod and I were thinking the same thing, watching that movie after supper." Dana put her hands together and pleaded with Hope to join them.

"How can I turn down an offer like that?" Hope grinned and followed her cousin back to the ranch, not noticing how Skeeter had perked up when she'd agreed to join them, or that Tony had scowled.

Two days later Hope was still thinking about the movie and the sermon. Not to mention Tony. While he didn't sit next to her, he was in the chair next to the sofa she sat on. And she had noticed that he kept his right side facing her as much as possible. Was it because of how she'd reacted the first time she'd seen his scars? Probably. Which only made her feel rotten.

She wanted to do something nice for Tony, but she didn't know what she could do. And she didn't want to single him out, because that would make it very obvious she was feeling sorry for him.

It wasn't so much that she felt sorry for the man, it was more that she felt guilty over her reaction, and Hope didn't want him thinking that she thought less of him for his injury. In fact, the more time she spent around him, the more she was in awe over him. She'd never met someone with such obvious injuries before. Tony seemed to be dealing quite well with his situation.

And the cowboy was cute.

He was a real cowboy too. Someone who'd grown up on a ranch. Biscuits and gravy, the man had a lot going for him. Not only was he handsome, but he was educated. And he was an Army officer. If Hope wasn't careful, she'd lose her heart over the man, and she wasn't even interested in dating right now.

"What's that serious face for?" Lottie Hamilton stood at the table holding a pot of hot coffee where Hope was drinking a mid-morning cup. Lottie owned the Frenchtown Roasting Company and had recently married Cove Hamilton, a now-retired rodeo star. The couple were practically Frenchtown royalty. And Hope had always liked Lottie and her little girl, Quinn.

"Oh, just thinking." Hope finished the last of her coffee.

"Care for a top off?" Lottie held out the hot pot of delicious, roasted coffee that made Hope sigh.

"That would be wonderful, thank you." Once her cup was full, Hope sniffed the aroma and sighed. "I don't know how you do it, but your coffee always makes me feel better." Hints of chicory, hazelnut, chocolate, and cinnamon wafted up to her. She added milk and sugar and began to sip her way to bliss.

"Thank you. I love roasting my own beans and trying different flavors. I'm glad you like this one. Not too many have liked it today. I don't think the chicory is a favorite." This was Lottie's first-time using chicory in her roasted coffee.

"It reminds me a little bit of a trip I took to New Orleans a few years ago. Usually, people add warm milk to the chicory coffee." Hope took another sip and smiled.

"Hm." Lottie tapped a finger on the coffee pot. "Sounds like I should try making a café au lait with this blend and see how that goes."

"Oh, yes, please. I'll take one to go." With a shrug, Hope decided more caffeine for the day would be a good thing. She had a lot of work to get to when she made it back to her aunt and uncle's farm. They were harvesting the rest of the corn that day, and then the next day they were going to start pulling in the green beans.

Even though they had equipment to help, there was still a lot of back-breaking work to do. She wasn't looking forward to the next week when they started pulling in the different berries and began making jams and jellies. Hope would rather be outside working then inside canning. But it was necessary to get the fruit canned right away. At least the vegetables canned easier than the jams.

As Hope walked out of the coffee shop, sipping her wonderful café au lait, she decided she'd need to go back and get a bag of those beans to make her own at home. Which was when she ran into the one man she didn't need to see—Tony Sullivan.

Chapter 8

The last woman Tony needed to see was right in his way. He'd come to town with Jerod to pick up supplies, and they decided to head over to the coffee shop for a treat before heading back to the ranch. Jerod was partial to the cinnamon rolls, and it was always easy to get him to stop in to the Frenchtown Roasting Company whenever someone mentioned cinnamon rolls.

"Hey, Lottie. How's it going?" Jerod greeted the proprietress as they entered.

Lottie turned toward them and smiled. "Welcome, Jerod. It's good to see you both."

Tony just about turned and walked out when the blonde in front of them turned around smiling.

"Hope, it's good to see you." Jerod grinned and shook her hand.

The cowgirl was holding a to-go cup of coffee, and Tony couldn't understand why she was back in line. His heart skipped a beat, and he scolded himself for reacting to the pretty lady. He was never going to win anyone's heart, so why would he even think about a woman that way? Especially one as pretty as Hope Lowry.

Tony was short for a man, only five feet eight inches, which was why he always wore cowboy boots; they added an extra inch to his short frame. But Hope was the perfect height for him. When they stood next to each other, she came up to his nose. All she had to do was tip her head up, and it would be so easy to take her lips in a sweet kiss.

That thought did much more than make his heart skip a beat. "Mucking the stalls." All he could do was think of something disgusting to get that image out of his head. It would do no one any good if he kept that line of thought going.

Hope furrowed her brows. "Huh?"

Heat seared its way up Tony's neck and into his face. He had to come up with something quick to explain what he'd just said.

Jerod chuckled and patted his shoulder. "I think Tony was just thinking about what he's got next on his schedule for today." He looked at Tony and grinned. "Weren't you, buddy?"

Jerod's save was going to cost him, and Tony knew it. "Yup, that's it, boss."

When Jerod winked at him, Tony knew what he would be doing when they got back. It didn't matter that it was all-hands-on-deck to try and make something of their float. The parade was only a couple of days away, and they were so far from having something decent to showcase in front of the entire town and all of its visitors.

While Tony knew the summer flower festival and Fourth of July parade did a lot for the town, in that moment he wished they weren't doing anything special for the holiday, or summer. But that was him being selfish. He'd heard the story about the Big Sky Christmas Tree Farm and how they almost went belly-up last Christmas. Cody Makinaw had needed the money from the various events he'd planned all year to coincide with the tourists coming to town in order to keep his farm in the family.

"Lucky you." Hope rolled her eyes and turned back to the counter when it was her turn to order. "Hi, Anise, can I get a pound of that chicory blend that Lottie just made?"

The barista was speechless and just stared.

Hope waved a hand. "Hello? Are you alright?"

Anise shook her head. "Sorry, but did you say you wanted a pound of the chicory blend coffee? Really?" She squinted and tilted her head.

"Have you tried it as a café au lait? The hot milk blends all of the flavors together in a way that just screams deliciousness. You should try it." Even though they were in Montana, Hope doubted that she had been the only one in town to ever visit New Orleans. It was a top destination place, and add in the eeriness of their history, and surely some of the locals had gone there for some fun.

"Ah, alright. I'll give it a try." Anise didn't sound very convinced, but she went and poured a one-pound bag of the whole beans.

Hope had purchased enough of their freshly roasted beans that Anise knew Hope would grind the beans herself as she needed them. While Hope would prepare coffee with pre-ground beans, she preferred to grind them herself whenever possible. The fresh grinds had the most flavor in them. And the flavor was what drinking coffee was all about, right? Well, that and the caffeine jolt.

Tony was wondering what she was talking about when Jerod asked, "What's the new blend?"

Dana would usually bring them all the new coffee blends after she worked a shift, but he didn't think they had anything with chicory in it, did they? Maybe it something Lottie only did that day?

When Hope turned around, the excitement on her face and in her voice caught Tony's attention, and he decided then and there to try that café au lait she was talking up.

Jerod ordered the same, along with two pans of Lottie's famous cinnamon rolls to bring back for everyone. "I know this will help the guys get moving. Nothing better to give you energy than a great dose of sugary dough."

"And don't forget the coffee," Anise added.

"Dana brought a couple of pounds back yesterday, so we have plenty back at the ranch. But I'm interested in this new drink Hope has." Jerod paid for his purchase and thanked Anise.

Both men stood to the side to wait for their order. The first part was the drinks, and while Tony wasn't normally a café au lait drinker—he preferred plain coffee with cream and sugar—he was pleasantly surprised by the flavors of the new coffee. Hope had been right, the hot milk mixed well with the beans, and it tasted like a drink he'd had one Christmas while in Iraq.

He and Jerod had decided not to bring back this particular blend since Jerod wasn't a fan. They figured most of the guys wouldn't care for it.

"Hey, Jerod, look." Tony pointed to two of the older cowboys in the coffee shop and watched as they drank their café au laits. "They like it. You're probably the only one who doesn't have discerning tastebuds when it comes to coffee."

They teased each other as they left the shop with their goodies, and Tony couldn't help but notice that Hope was still in town. Her beat-up blue truck was sitting outside of the general store. The entire ride back to the Crooked Arrow, he couldn't help but think about her and how her face lit up over something so insignificant as coffee. Some people did take delight in the little things, but others didn't. Tony liked the fact that Hope seemed the type to enjoy the simple things of life.

When Tony and Jerod walked into the barn, the place was in turmoil. Skeeter was yelling for someone to do something, and Rogue was barking at Dixon, which was an unusual event. The dog rarely barked, even when someone knocked at the front door. Sam was standing off to the side laughing, and Dana just threw her hands in the air.

"Did someone order a coffee break?" Jerod bellowed when no one even noticed their arrival.

If that hadn't gotten everyone's attention, the captain would have begun barking out orders. Even though none of them were still in the service, they all had it drilled in them to obey commands. And since Tony as the only officer in the group, they'd listen if he spoke up. He almost wanted to yell, "Drop and give me twenty," but he knew that some of the guys would have difficultly doing push-ups, and he didn't want to make anyone feel bad for not being able to do one.

Which got him to thinking, could Sam do push-ups? The former soldier was missing most of his left arm. In its place was a prosthetic made of hard plastic and stainless steel. Tony watched the man corral his dog, who was off-duty by the looks of things—his vest was nowhere in sight. Maybe they had all started playing a game that had gotten out of hand? Either way, it put a smile on Tony's face as he watched everyone squirm under Jerod's gaze.

"What in tarnation is going on here?" Jerod plopped the boxes full of doughy goodness down on a table to the right of the entrance and looked to Sam.

The man who'd been there almost as long as Jerod had put both of his hands in the air and shook his head. "Don't look at me. It was all her fault." He pointed to a woman that Tony liked and hadn't seen in over a week.

"I'm sorry. I should have known that taking Buffy and Spike off duty as soon as they saw Rogue would be a mistake." Nelly Wilson, the resident dog whisperer and service dog trainer, had put a leash on one of her dogs, the black lab with white spots on his head, also known as Spike.

The other dog, oddly enough, was looking right at Tony. If he wasn't mistaken, that was Buffy. She rarely liked men, but he was the exception to the rule it seemed. Buffy was a chocolate lab that always came to him looking for some loving, as long as she was off duty. And since Nelly hadn't put Buffy's service dog vest back on, the dog must have thought she was free to do as she wanted.

Buffy pranced over to greet Tony, and she rubbed up against his right leg. When Tony leaned down to pet her, she lifted her head and licked his face.

"Ah, Buffy." Tony chuckled and wiped the dog's drool off his cheek. "I know you love me, girl, but come on." He leaned down and rubbed the top of her head, even though he didn't want to support her licking his face.

The rest of the group got quiet, and when Tony lifted his head, he noticed that he and Buffy were the center of attention. "What? I don't like my face licked. Is there something wrong with that?" He wasn't sure what had caused everyone in the room to stare at him, but they were.

And he was getting uncomfortable.

Nelly walked over with Spike on his leash. "Tony, nice to see you again." Then she looked down at Buffy who sat back on her haunches and waited for Nelly to give her a command. "*Braver hund*, Buffy." The dog wagged her tail but stayed put while Nelly put her vest on and attached the leash.

"Do the dogs really understand when their vests go on that they're back on the clock?" Tony had seen Rogue and Sam practice various things with Nelly on occasion, but he had never stayed around to watch much since he wasn't in line for a dog.

Nelly stood up straight and looked at Tony. "Care to help me with some training this week? I can show you how they work and play."

Tony was about to say no, but then he stopped for a second and thought about it. Jerod had asked the guys if any would be interested in working with Nelly and her dogs, helping them to train with wounded vets for their future partners. Tony hadn't really thought about it, but since the Sunday sermon, he was thinking that it might be a good idea to help out where he could.

Maybe God had a reason for why Buffy liked him but none of the other guys? Nelly had said Buffy would only be paired up with a woman since she had an issue with men. Buffy's affection toward him must mean something. Was it God saying this was a way he could give back?

"Sure, why not? But we've got to get this float finished before I can think about anything else." Tony sighed when he looked at the flatbed trailer; despite the hours of work put in by the vets today already, it didn't look much different from earlier that morning.

"Yeah, that's partly why I'm here." The dog trainer pointed to the box she'd brought with her.

"What's in it?" In only a couple of steps, Tony was standing next to the box full of stuffed dogs.

"Sam thought it might make more sense to change the float into something a little bit simpler than your original design. Instead of representing all lines of service in flowers, he thought that you"—Nelly looked to Jerod —"might appreciate doing a float showing off service dogs."

The idea was good, but what did a bunch of stuffed animals have to do with service dogs? Tony was about to voice his thought when Skeeter did.

"I get having the dogs on the float, but the kids' toys?" Skeeter scratched his chin. "What are those for?"

A grin spread across Nelly's face. "I was thinking if you guys were on the float with the dogs, some of the stuffed animals could be used for decorations, but some could be used to throw out to the kids lining the street."

"Won't that be expensive?" Costs were all Tony could think of ever since he'd learned the ranch wasn't doing so well financially.

"Actually, the stuffed animals were donated to me last year. I haven't had an opportunity to use them for anything, so I brought them with me. I was thinking the larger ones could be used to decorate the float, and some of the small ones could be thrown at to the kids, instead of candy."

"Whoa, now. We have a boatload of candy to give out. And one box of toys won't be enough." Skeeter eyed the box warily. It was a large box, but there definitely wasn't enough toys there to take the place of candy.

Jerod scratched his chin. "I don't know. I heard we had a rat come in and take a bunch of our candy. I doubt we have enough to give everyone now." He arched an eyebrow, looking pointedly at Skeeter.

"Hey, now." Skeeter put his hands up. "No one told me we couldn't have that candy in the store room. I thought it was for everyone to enjoy."

"The sign said, 'Hands off.' Please explain how that meant it was for everyone to enjoy?" Dana crossed her arms over her chest and glared at him. Skeeter might be a grown man, but he acted like a teenager more often than not.

"What sign? I didn't see no stinkin' sign." Skeeter put a hand over his mouth to hide his grin, but everyone knew he was smiling.

Jerod put a hand up to get everyone's attention. "Alright. I like the idea. Nelly, tell me more."

Chapter 9

The night before the parade, Dana invited Hope over for dinner with everyone at the ranch. Nelly had brought her dogs with her, and the pack of them were stretched out on the living room rug.

"So, let me get this straight," Hope said during dessert. "You decided at the last minute to change the entire design of your float? And tonight you want to finish off the last of the decorations and then do some sort of walk-through with the dogs?" Hope thought they were going to need more than the evening to finish a float they'd only had a couple of days to re-do.

"I know, it sounds crazy, but the design is very simple. You'll see." Nelly ate the last bite of her peach cobbler and sat back with a satisfied look on her face. "I think this is going to be a lot of fun."

Uncertain, but not wanting to rain on anyone's parade, Hope ate the rest of her dessert in silence, eager to get outside and see the float. When everyone at the table started getting up, excitement bubbled in her stomach.

Either the float would be cool, or it would be a nightmare. Only time would tell.

"Okay, Hope, wait here. I'll have someone come get you once it's all set." Jerod grinned and trotted off after the guys.

When Nelly went after them, Hope wondered what in the world was going on. Why would she be the only one to stay behind? She sat on the back patio biting her nails and debating if she should continue to sit there all alone or make her way to the barn. When she realized she would spoil their surprise after all their hard work, she relaxed and decided to enjoy the cool summer air.

The temperature had been steadily climbing the past week, and most of the time Hope was dripping with sweat if she stayed outside for very long. But tonight, she didn't need to worry about wearing a hat with a sweatband or getting hat head. The breeze that came in off the forest behind the ranch helped cool everything off.

If Hope wasn't mistaken, they'd get a nice summer storm in a day or two. Hopefully, it would wait until after tomorrow's Fourth of July festivities. She knew everyone, from the ranchers to the farmers, would welcome a good rain. As long as it didn't come down so hard it destroyed crops, everyone would be happy, even if it was only enough to water the crops one day. Any and all water was welcomed in the summer.

As she sat there looking up at the stars beginning to peak out from the darkening sky, she missed that someone had left the barn and was heading her way. When she looked down, she almost groaned. Skeeter was a nice enough guy, but she wasn't into his flirtatious manner.

"Hey there, pretty lady. I think everyone is ready if you are?" Skeeter took off his hat and held it directly in front of him as he waited for Hope.

"Thanks. So, can you tell me anything about this float?" While Hope would have preferred Dana coming out to get her, or even Nelly, it was fitting that one of the veterans of the Crooked Arrow escorted her to the barn.

Right before she reached the barn, the large doors flew open. "Ta-da!" A smile as wide as the Mississippi River spread across Dana's face as she waved Hope inside.

"Someone sure does seem happy..." Hope's mouth dropped open when she stepped inside.

The long flatbed trailer normally used to haul cars and trucks sat in the middle of the barn floor. The outside rim, which had been just a series of buckets and a sparse collection of flowers the last time she'd seen it, was packed with colorful blooms. There were even stuffed animal dogs peeking out from the petals. In the back of the float was a large sign, similar to the entrance posts of the Crooked Arrow. Along the top it read, "Crooked Arrow Ranch" and just underneath was a hanging sign with the words, "Where the Light Overcomes the Darkness."

In front of the sign stood Tony with Buffy the dog. In front of them were Sam and Rogue, Mike Blankenship and Angel, then Arthur Landbury and Spike. In the very front stood the rest of the guys from the ranch, including Skeeter who had jumped up the moment he'd run into the barn.

Hope put a hand to her heart and felt tears prick behind her eyes.

The men were wearing their uniforms, something Hope had missed when Skeeter had come to escort her to the barn. Her gaze had been mostly on the sky, then the barn, and she'd barely even looked at him. Wearing their service vests, the dogs stood with the same military alertness as their partners. They were gruff, injured, and hurting, but they stood at attention, ready and waiting for orders.

"Wow, this looks…" Hope was speechless for a second. "It's fantastic. Great job everyone." Hope walked around the float and noticed the flowers in more detail. Some seemed to showcase the different military branch insignias. "Very clever."

Without meaning to, Hope looked up and locked eyes with Tony. The intensity in his gaze sent shivers down her spine. His throat bobbed up and down as though he was fighting it.

Could it be that he felt the connection, too? Hope needed to break the connection. But oh, did she want to feel those emotions again. She missed having a partner in life. But the next time man she chose would be a God-fearing one. And someone she knew would be healthy for her heart, and her life.

"I know, I can't believe they were able to get this done so quickly, and so beautifully," Dana added. "Now, I wish I was going to be on the float."

Jerod walked up and put an arm around his wife. "If you want to be in the tractor with me as I pull the float, you're welcome to sit on my lap." He grinned suggestively at his wife.

Hope laughed and shook her head. "Newlyweds."

"I'm tempted, but I don't think the kids would enjoy seeing me on your lap." Dana winked at her husband and leaned up to kiss his cheek.

"Oh, get a room." Skeeter covered his eyes and groaned. "When are they going to get over the honeymoon phase?"

"Never, I hope," Jerod teased.

Wanting to change the subject and get back on track, Hope cleared her throat. "Well, does this mean your float is all ready to go tomorrow?" She looked at the floor of the float and frowned. "Where are all the bags of candy?"

Dana glared at Skeeter. "Someone couldn't keep his grubby little paws off it so I had to hide it. I'll bring it out and put it in the boxes right before the parade starts."

"Hey, I only had a few." Skeeter didn't look the least bit ashamed of his actions.

"You mean a few bags?" Tony chuckled and shook his head. "I saw you sitting on the edge of the float just yesterday with at least fifty candy wrappers at your feet."

Skeeter crossed his arms over his chest and grumbled. Hope couldn't understand what he'd said, but she figured it was something similar to what a teenaged boy might say.

"Well, I, for one, am very excited to see you guys drive down Main Street tomorrow." Hope smiled. "This should be a lot of fun."

She and Dana made arrangements to meet and sit together tomorrow morning while they waited for the parade to start.

Then Hope said her goodbyes and left with a huge smile on her face. She was really and truly excited for the parade. It had been ages since she'd been to one. Memories of the times she'd spent in Frenchtown assailed her, and the entire drive home she sang along to Faith Hill's CD as it blared through her speakers.

The next morning, right after getting her chores done, Hope grabbed a thermos of fresh coffee, a few snacks for the day, and a folding chair before she headed out to meet Dana. They had decided to try and get a spot as close to the Frenchtown Roasting Company as possible. That way they could head inside whenever they needed anything without missing too much of the festivities.

Sadly, most of the town had had the same idea.

"I can't believe we have to sit outside the one office building we have here in town." Dana laughed. "At least they have nice restrooms."

"True. And really, we aren't too far from the vendor carts. In fact"—Hope stood up—"I think I'm gonna go and get us both a snow cone. What flavor do you want?"

By the time the parade started, both were full of junk food and ready for a nap. The sun beat down on them, and even though a nice breeze was billowing again, there wasn't a cloud in the sky. Nothing to break the sun's stark rays. Nothing, that is, except their sunglasses and large hats.

So much for the reports of a possible rainstorm coming through town.

It was after three in the afternoon and everyone in town was practically screaming with excitement over the first of the marching bands. "I can't believe we were the lucky ones to get the University of Montana marching band this year. Isn't there a contest to get them to come to a town's parade?" Hope had attended UM and knew their band was popular across the entire state and beyond.

"I think they can usually squeeze in three parades a day, if they're close. The school looks at who's having a parade and the times, then they schedule. But yeah, there is also some sort of lottery involved. This isn't our first time getting them, but it has been a while since they came to our parade." Dana jumped up and down yelling, "Go Grizzlies!"

Most of the residents of Montana who went to college attended the University of Montana and were proud Grizzlies. Hope noticed quite a few Grizzly pennants and large foam fingers among the crowd. At one time she'd had one of those large, dark red foam fingers with a bear's paw print on the palm and the upraised finger that said, "Griz Nation." She grinned as the last of the one-hundred-and-forty-member band made its way past her. Thoughts of where they were off to next flitted through her head and disappeared the moment she saw the tiny cars driven by the Shriners in their funny costumes.

The group of men who coordinated the Frenchtown parade were older and loved to ride in flying carpets. They weren't actually flying carpets, but they looked every inch like they'd flown out of *Aladdin*. The colorful fringe that surrounded each vehicle matched that of the burgundy in the Grizzly band uniform. Even their hats were burgundy with navy-blue tassels to match the university's colors.

In fact, Hope noticed quite a few people wearing UM shirts and hats. She had one in her closet but hadn't thought to wear it. She wished she'd have done that instead of the "Cowgirl Up" T-shirt she wore today. It was a turquoise blue to match the side accents of her cowgirl boots she only wore on special occasions.

"How far back will the ranch's float be?" Hope wondered aloud.

"I think they are about halfway through the parade." Dana looked down to see what was coming next. The first float of the parade was the high school prom queen and her court from just a few weeks ago. The queen was wearing a pink frilly dress and a tiara that would be passed on to the next prom queen the following May. Until then, this prom queen would be invited to attend multiple events throughout the year, including the Christmas pageant. She sure would get a lot of use out of the tiara and title.

"Oh, look!" Hope pointed to the group behind the prom queen. "Is that our high school band? They're so cute in their uniforms." She cooed and clapped as the tiny marching band passed by. They sounded every bit as good as the university band.

The crowd went wild with all of the excitement. The next three floats threw candy and some cheap, plastic necklaces. The kids in the crowd ran out and grabbed all the loot they could.

Then, when the Crooked Arrow Ranch float was in sight, both women began jumping and hollering for the float. A little girl next to Hope clapped and pointed at the dogs.

Suddenly, the float stopped in the middle of the street, and Hope turned to Dana. "Is something wrong?"

Dana chuckled. "Just watch."

Her breathe left her when she noticed that all of the dogs were laying down except for the one with Tony. "Isn't that Buffy with Tony?"

No one responded to Hope's question, so she kept looking and noticed Tony say something. He pointed his hand down and held it in front of Buffy's nose. He gave what looked like a treat to the dog. Then he said another command. It was too bad it was so loud, because she was hoping to hear the commands that he had learned for this parade.

"Is he…?" Hope put a hand over her mouth as she watched in awe as Buffy Army-crawled from the back of the float to the front. Then Tony said something else, and Buffy returned for another treat.

The crowd went wild, but the dogs remained calm, keeping a keen eye on everyone. Smiling, the veterans threw some stuffed dogs into the crowd. The little girl next to Hope jumped up and screamed loudly for a toy.

Tony noticed the girl and smiled at her, then at Hope. He leaned down, picked up a stuffed dog from the box next to his feet, and threw it at them. The dog landed right in Hope's hands, and she held it up for everyone to see.

When the little girl didn't get one, she sniffled and rubbed her eyes. Then she turned puppy-dog eyes at Hope.

"Oh, I'm sorry. I bet they meant for this to go to you." Hope handed the little girl the dog and smiled at her.

The girl's mom shook her head and tried to give the dog back to Hope. "You got it fair and square. It should be yours."

"That's alright. I know those guys, I'm sure I can get another one later. Let your daughter enjoy the toy." Hope patted the little girl's head, and her smile radiated all of the joy an eight-year-old could muster.

"That's really nice of you, thank you." The mom put a hand over her heart, and Hope noticed tears at the edge of her eyes.

Her response was cut off by the emotion welling up in her chest, so Hope could only nod.

When the next group, the high school football team, walked by, everyone's attention went back to the parade.

Chapter 10

"Buffy, did you see that? She gave it away." Tony waved at Hope and the little girl as they passed by. He turned his head to the other side, waved, and picked up another little stuffed dog to throw. It looked very similar to Buffy with its chocolate-colored coat and loving eyes. "Look, it's you."

Buffy sniffed the little toy and nodded her head before focusing on the crowd. When Buffy gave a little chuff, Tony searched for who she was looking at. Thankfully, they were going so slow that it was easy for him to identify the child in a wheelchair, a US Army ballcap on his head. He did his best to aim the toy at the kid with the patriotic spirit.

When the toy landed right in the kid's lap, Tony couldn't help but do a fist pump. He grinned and waved at the kid, who returned his smile with a look of utter awe. It felt good to make a kid smile. He wondered if that was how Hope had felt when she'd given her stuffed dog to that little girl.

Buffy rubbed against his leg and pointed again to another kid. Tony picked up another toy and tossed it to the little boy in the heather-gray Grizzlies T-shirt. Then he waved at the kids, grabbed a handful of candy, and threw it out. This was turning out to be a lot of fun for both Tony and Buffy.

When they made it to the end of the route, Tony wanted to go again. "That was better than an e-ticket ride."

Skeeter gave him a funny look, but Jerod laughed and agreed. "It's nice to give back to the community, isn't it?"

"Yeah, it is. But it's even better when it's little kids, you know?" Tony had done more than his share of community service hours since arriving at the ranch, but he hadn't seen the way the kids' faces lit up with joy until that day. Most of what he'd done had been behind the scenes. Not that he wanted to be the center of attention, but maybe he could dress up as Santa next Christmas, or something, as a way to give more joy to kids.

"So, what's next?" Skeeter took a long drink of soda and looked expectantly at Jerod.

"Yeah, what else is happening? I see a lot of people still roaming around." Dixon scratched the stubble of his beard and looked out to see Lottie refilling her coffee cart.

"Well, once the last of the parade finishes up, then people will all go into the streets and help clean up any messes left behind." Jerod pointed to a mess left by one of the horses in the parade.

Mike scrunched his nose. "Really? You don't have a team who works for the city to come through and do clean up?" He furrowed his brow and thought about what he'd just said. "Never mind. I forgot we're in a one-horse town."

Everyone laughed at his attempt of a joke.

"I think there's more than one horse in this town. Did you mean one-light?" Tony grinned and pointed to the one signal light in town.

"Hardy-har-har. You know what I meant." Mike shook his head and chuckled.

"Alright, let's get this float to the lot down the road and make sure we return Nelly's dogs to her in good shape." The gleam in Jerod's eyes when he looked at everyone was enough to tell all the men that he was excited for the rest of the night.

Even though no one said anything, Tony knew there would be fireworks. Fourth of July celebrations always had fireworks. But he wasn't sure how he'd react. This would be the first time he'd experience them since the bombing.

When Tony had gone through his initial counseling sessions while still in the hospital, the counselor had warned him to stay away from loud noises, especially fireworks, for a while. There was no need to explain why. Tony had seen firsthand what happened to a soldier dealing with PTSD while he was still in the hospital.

One of the new nurses had dropped a tray. It was metal and made a very loud noise on the linoleum floor. Several of the men nearby screamed and cowered behind any large object they could find. One man even went so far as to overturn his bed and hunker down behind it. The nurse was in tears when she'd realized what she'd done.

While the noise made him jump and look around, he didn't feel the need to hide. Probably because he couldn't remember the sound of the explosion. What he did remember was the searing heat. Fire was still something he stayed clear of.

The memories of that day came back, and he felt himself stiffen up. His heart rate must have doubled, and his breathing was ragged. That was until he felt something nudge his leg and lick his hand. The warmth and affection broke him out of his nightmare, and he looked down to see two loving eyes looking back up at him.

"Buffy. How'd you know, girl?" Tony knelt down and scratched her between the ears. The dog was working, but he also knew from watching Sam and Rogue that it was alright if a wounded vet gave love and affection to a working dog. That was what they were there for, wasn't it? To give love and support to their partner.

Tony sucked in a breath. If Buffy, who usually didn't care for men, was loving on him, did that mean she was choosing him? But Tony knew he didn't need a service dog. He just needed more time to heal and process everything he'd gone through. He was nothing like how Sam had been, and sometimes still was.

In fact, if anyone at the ranch needed a service animal, it was probably Dixon. The man had a prosthetic leg and still suffered from PTSD. In fact, Tony wondered how Dixon was going to handle the fireworks that night. Maybe Buffy could help him?

As he was pondering how to help the man that night, Nelly walked up to him.

"I see Buffy has finally met a man she likes." Nelly leaned down and scratched behind one of the dog's ears. "*Braver hund*. You were such a good girl. I'm proud of you." Then she made her way to the rest of the dogs, ending with Rogue.

Tony watched Nelly and recognized the light in her eyes as love for the dogs, as well as her work. The dogs returned her love without reservation. They all wagged their tails like mad when she spoke to them. It was amazing how the dogs knew when they were working and when it was time to play. Their ability to understand German flabbergasted Tony. He could barely understand a few phrases in Spanish; he doubted he could learn anything more than "good girl" or *"Braver hund"* in German.

Sam seemed to be doing quite well with his training. Nelly hadn't just dumped Rogue with him and left. Of course, they were dating now, but still, she spent time several nights a week training him to speak the German commands while Rogue learned how to support Sam the best way he could. It was amazing to see how the human and the dog partnered, and the way the dog truly helped Sam was nothing short of miraculous.

In fact, Tony couldn't remember Sam laughing before he met Nelly and Rogue. Now, the man laughed several times a week. Tony was certain that it wouldn't be too long before Sam was laughing on a daily basis. The doctors had all told him laughter was the best medicine. If the way Sam was behaving lately was any indication, then those doctors were right.

Tony felt rather than saw when Hope and Dana joined them. Jerod's eyes brightened, so there was that little bit of evidence. But when Tony turned around and saw the smile on Hope's face, his maudlin thoughts turned to more enjoyable ones. He had a surprise for Hope, one he hoped she liked.

Buffy had instinctively stayed glued to Tony's left side, so the leash was in his left hand. He leaned over with his right hand and took the gift he had for Hope out of his pack and headed to where the cowgirl stood, looking breathtaking in her fancy boots, jeans, and T-shirt.

The sun was still high in the sky, but a cool breeze had begun to blow in some clouds, and some of the women, Hope included, had put on lightweight jackets. Hope's denim jacket matched her jeans and only added to the whole cowgirl look. Tony gulped when she turned her brilliant smile toward him.

"Tony, that was great. How'd you learn how to command Buffy like that?" Hope began to lean over to pet the dog, but then stood up and took a step back. "Sorry, she's still got her working vest on."

Nelly waved her hand. "That's alright. I'll take their vests off now. They could use some loving after how well they did on the float." She took off Spike's vest and gathered the other vests from the guys who had taken them off the dogs.

Tony held Buffy's vest in his right hand, hiding the gift he had for Hope. Once he handed the vest off to Nelly, he turned to Hope. "I saw how you gave your stuffed animal to that little girl. That was really sweet of you."

"I figured you meant for the toys to go to the kids. And when she turned her sad eyes on me, my heart broke for her." Hope shrugged as though it was no big deal.

"Well, I had meant it for you. But what you did was nice." Tony handed her the stuffed toy and smiled.

Wide eyes and a sweet smile greeted his gift. "For me? Really?" Hope took the little dog that looked like a cross between a German Shephard and a Poodle with white, fluffy fur.

"Yes, for you." Tony had to clear the emotion from his throat before he could say more.

"Thank you. This is really sweet of you." Hope held the animal to her chest and knew exactly where it would go in her room—on her bed in front of her pillows.

The two of them stared into each other's eyes. Tony felt the connection between them solidifying, and he wasn't sure what to do. This wasn't what he needed at the moment. Surely, Hope wouldn't be interested in him. He knew he looked like a monster when his hat was off and nothing to hide his scars. He still had another surgery, and he'd have more scars for a while after that. It would probably be a year, or more, before he'd know exactly how he would look. Healing after something like what he'd gone through wasn't easy, or fast. And he knew from the way his family reacted that no one would want him. How could they? He was a monster. But unlike the Beast in *Beauty and the Beast*, this was real life, not a fairytale, and no Belle would want him.

His connection with Hope broke when he felt a nudge against his thigh. Buffy was there, wagging her tail at Hope. Once Tony broke their connection, Hope looked down and smiled at Buffy.

"Hey, girl. You did a great job out there." Hope leaned over and rubbed the dog's head. Buffy leaned into her lovingly and closed her eyes. One of her back legs began to twitch and a guttural sound of contentment rumbled from her throat.

He couldn't help it; Tony laughed and shook his head. "I see Buffy really does prefer women to men." He couldn't blame the dog. He'd be in heaven if Hope loved on him too.

Tony shook his head to get that thought out of there. "Sooo, what's next?"

Hope popped up and grinned. "Dinner. There's a big barbecue at the Baptist church. Everyone's welcome to join in. And all of the money raised goes toward their benevolence fund to help people in need throughout the year."

"Well, that sounds like a great idea." Tony looked to Jerod, who nodded. Then he looked to the rest of the guys. "You all game?"

"Oh, yeah!" Skeeter exclaimed. "You know I never turn down barbecue."

"Don't you mean you never turn down food?" Dana rolled her eyes heavenward.

If Skeeter had his way, every night would be barbecue steaks or ribs. The guy could really pack away the meat. Tony didn't know how he could eat so much and never gain an ounce. "Why am I not surprised?" Tony chuckled and headed toward the church.

The great thing about Frenchtown was that most everything was within walking distance if you were already on Main Street, even if you were at the far end like they were. Even so, Tony found Dixon wincing. The man was still learning how to deal with his new gait.

"Dixon, what do you say we take the van?" Jerod pointed to a community van that was cruising slowly down the street.

"I don't want special treatment." Dixon tried to walk away from the van, but Jerod clapped his shoulder.

"It's for anyone who wants a lift," Dana added. "I'm tired from being out in the sun all day." She put her hand up, and the van stopped.

"I'll drive over and meet you there with our gear." Hope walked back toward where they had stashed their chairs and other items from the long day.

For just a moment, Tony considered asking Hope for a lift, but thought better of it. He still had Buffy's leash in his hand and noticed Nelly and Sam were walking with the rest of the dogs. He decided it would be best to follow them and let Buffy get in a walk while she could.

Chapter 11

As Hope walked toward her truck, she looked back over her shoulder and noticed Tony following after Nelly and Sam. The couple must have been in their own little world because they seemed to be ignoring everyone around them, including the dogs.

Well, maybe they weren't ignoring the dogs exactly, but their attention was definitely focused on each other. She could understand. Her last boyfriend had taken all of her time and attention. It was too much, and some had even called it codependency. Maybe it was. Either way, Nelly and Sam did seem to have a healthy relationship. They each did things without the other and were rarely alone.

While some might call walking to the barbecue being alone, it wasn't. Not really. Besides, Tony seemed to be their chaperone. He was only about ten feet behind them with Buffy. A part of her wanted to invite Tony and Buffy to ride with her, but then she thought better of it. While she enjoyed Tony's company, and thought he was quite handsome, no matter his scars, she wasn't in a position to have a healthy relationship.

And from the one comment Dana had made, neither was he.

So, she drove by herself to the church for the barbecue. She knew from past experience it would be fantastic. The vast majority of the town would be there, as would a lot of visitors. The flower festival had ended yesterday, so those left in town only had this event, or their hotel, to choose from. And who wouldn't be excited about some good ol' barbecued meat from local ranches? This was the epitome of a western meal.

She was already thinking about Mrs. McCullough's cheesy mac 'n' cheese. Just the memory of barbecued pork and short ribs had her stomach gurgling in anticipation. This was going to be the sort of night where she had to be rolled home, like that blue girl in *Willy Wonka and the Chocolate Factory*. Unlike the kids in the story, Hope had permission to eat everything in sight. Right after she paid her ten dollars. While it might seem expensive, when you considered all the food and drinks that would be available, it was a steal. And besides, the money went to a good cause.

Her aunt had baked huckleberry pies for the occasion. All of the food and accompaniments were donated, from the potato salad to the plastic forks. And the men of the church usually fought over who got to do the honors at the grill. It seemed Frenchtown had multiple aspiring grill masters. Shoot, she'd pay double, no triple, the amount just to get a slice of Mrs. Masters's six-layer chocolate cake. Oh, just thinking about cake make her mouth water.

She made it just in time to hear the pastor finish saying grace for the meal. Hope found Dana and the crew and got in line with them. Somehow, they were pretty close to the front. "Say, how'd you get such a great spot in line?" She turned her head and looked back to see a line a mile long.

A cheese-eating grin met her inquiring eyes. "It seems that veterans and the elderly get to cut the line." Dana waggled her brows and looked ahead to see that they were next to get a plate.

"Should I go to the back of the line? I'm not a veteran." A little bit of guilt replaced the tummy rumbles, and Hope started to get out of line.

"You've been with us all day. I think it's fine that you're here and not back there." Dana pointed to the end of the snaking line. "Besides, if you went back there, we'd be all done before you even got served."

"Are you sure? I feel bad." Hope bit her lower lip.

"I'm not a veteran, and no one questioned me when I came up here. Did anyone question you?" When Dana picked up a plate, she handed it back to Hope.

Hope quirked a brow and waited a moment. "Uh, you're married to the veteran who runs the local ranch that's here just for wounded vets. No one is going to bat an eye at you getting the benefits that a veteran does."

"And you're family." Dana shrugged and put her plate out for barbecued spareribs.

Realizing that it was useless to argue, Hope joined her cousin and thanked the old man who served her the best-smelling meat she could ever remember. "Thank you, this looks fantastic."

"It should be, we slow-cooked it all morning before putting it on the grill." The old man gave her a toothy smile and waved her down the line.

By the time she was done, her plate was overloaded with all sorts of homemade goodness. She had to put her plate down on the table and go back for desert and drinks. When she came back, she noticed that Tony was seated next to her. She didn't notice he had been sitting there when she'd put her plate down.

Then she saw the smile that went from ear to ear on her meddling cousin's face and knew exactly what the sneaky woman was up to. Matchmaking wasn't something Hope needed at the moment. In fact, she needed it as much as she needed a pet skunk.

Once Hope was seated with her napkin in her lap, she tentatively looked at Tony out of the corner of her eye. He was eating slowly. And she noticed that he sat on her left; he must have wanted to keep her from seeing his scars again. A twinge of regret spiked up her back as she remembered how rude she'd been when she saw his face that first time.

"So, are you having fun today?" Tony asked before taking a bite of the mac 'n' cheese.

Before Hope could say anything, Tony practically moaned in appreciation of the cheesy goodness.

"It's good, right?" After that, Hope and Tony had no problems talking about the food, or the parade. In fact, the conversation flowed so well that when she ate the last bite on her plate, she hadn't even realized it was all gone.

All Hope had left was the chocolate cake. She knew from past experience that it was best enjoyed with a mug of hot coffee. "I'm going to get a coffee, would you like one?"

Tony looked from the giant cake in front of Hope to the small piece of huckleberry pie in front of him. "Sure, thank you."

When Hope came back with two steaming hot cups, she noticed that someone had taken a rather large bite out of her cake. She eyed her cousin with suspicion, but her cousin seemed oblivious. Dana was busy talking with Jerod and Dixon.

Mike, who sat on her right side, was staring at his almost-empty plate with a hand over his stomach. "I don't think I can eat another bite."

So that left Tony. Hope stared daggers at the man, who only looked back at her with a grateful smile when she handed him his cup of coffee.

"Who ate my cake?" Hope demanded.

"Uh..." Tony pointed to the still giant piece on her paper plate. "It's right there."

"Uh-huh. And it's missing a huge bite." She sat down and glared at the man.

He pretended not to hear her, which only made her even more suspicious. Hope looked at his face but couldn't see any chocolate. Then she studied his shirt and picked something up off the collar. "What's this?"

Tony turned to look at the piece of cake in her fingers. "Looks like huckleberry pie." He grinned.

She couldn't help but laugh when he looked so innocent. "I see how it is." She took her fork and stabbed it into his pie and quickly brought the stolen morsel to her mouth. It really was a great pie, but she could get one any time she wanted. The chocolate cake was only available during special town events. And sometimes it was all gone by the time she got to the front of the line. In fact, Hope hadn't had any of Mrs. Masters's six-layer chocolate cake in at least three years.

"Hey, that's mine." Tony pulled his remaining piece of pie closer to his body and protected it with his arms. "You've got that giant piece of cake still to eat."

"It's not so giant after you took a piece." Hope arched a brow and waited for him to deny it.

Instead, Tony smiled and shrugged. "You snooze, you lose."

Shaking her head, Hope couldn't be mad at the guy. He was right. She had been the one to walk away and leave her cake unattended. She'd remember next time.

Several hours later, as the sun was making its final goodbye for the night, and the moon's small crescent was trying to take over and light the summer sky, an announcement came about the fireworks.

"Well, that's my signal to head home. Anyone else want to go back before the sky explodes?" Dixon looked to the group who had left the dining table behind and were now all sitting a fair distance from a bonfire out by the edge of the empty field.

When it was warm, the field was where most of the town's events were held. The rodeos set up shop here as well as the carnival. And when they had events like the parade, vendors would set up and sell drinks and wares while everyone waited for the firework display. Bonfires even spotted the edges of the field, still far enough away from any brush or trees to be safe.

When Hope was a teenager, she'd been part of a group of other kids who enjoyed staying close to the fire. There was usually a cute boy, or two, she wanted to talk with. Or even flirt when the chance arose. But this year, she was happy to sit with Dana and the guys from the Crooked Arrow. They all shared stories about how they celebrated the holiday in their youth. None of them spoke about celebrating while on the battlefield. And Hope wondered what, if anything, the military did to mark the day for the troops in battle. Was that when some of the famous singers ended up doing USO tours? Did Tony ever see anyone exciting in concert while he was overseas? These questions and more were on the tip of her tongue, but never made it past her lips.

Hope wasn't sure what the rules where when it came to asking questions about how someone spent their time in war. She knew enough to not ask how many kills anyone had. That was the last thing a civilian should even think about. However, it was a question she'd had when she'd first met Jerod. She knew his background was in special operations and just knew he had a kill list.

Instead, she'd asked him where he'd been stationed overseas. After receiving a vague response, she changed the subject and never asked him questions about his time in Iraq or Afghanistan. And as much as she wanted to know about Tony's experience, she had decided not to ask him any questions. He had been injured in a bombing and probably was still trying to heal, mentally as well as physically. She could see the physical scars from the bomb, but what about the emotional scars? Would she be able to see any signs of those?

Then, when Dixon got up to leave, Hope looked around at their group and noticed Skeeter joining him. That surprised her. She expected the flirtatious young man to stick around and see who he could meet.

"I'll be happy to take anyone back now and then I'll come back here for the rest of the night with y'all." Jerod pulled keys from his pocket and left with the two men.

When Tony stayed put, Hope smiled inwardly. She'd wondered if he would leave early and was secretly glad he was staying for the rest of the festivities. Not that she expected him to sit with her, or anything, but it would be nice if she could find a way to spend more time with him.

Once Jerod and the two guys had left, someone turned up the volume on the radio, and a fun Garth Brooks song got a lot of people up and dancing. "Come on, join me." Hope called out to Dana. When she did, the remaining guys from the ranch joined the two women. Then Sam and Nelly joined in as well.

The four dogs barked along with the tune and everyone laughed at their obvious enjoyment of the music.

Rogue came up next to Sam and did a little squirmy move that almost looked like dancing.

Then Buffy came up next to Tony and proceeded to nudge him enough to get the cowboy dancing next to Hope. Was the dog actually trying to play matchmaker? Or did she just like Hope and want to be closer to her? Hope wasn't sure what the motives were, but she wasn't going to look a gift horse in the mouth. She smiled at Buffy and took Tony's hand as the music slowed.

The next song to come over the speakers was "Friends in Low Places." The entire town began singing and waltzing along with the song. Even Tony knew the little dip that was always done during the "low places" part of the song.

After the special third verse had been belted out by everyone present, and the song ended, Hope had to stop and take a drink. Her breathing was labored, but she couldn't stop smiling. This day had been one of the best she'd had in so long. Even all her time with Billy hadn't been nearly as fun as this day had been. And it wasn't even over yet.

It was just about time for the fireworks to start, and Jerod had just made it back, out of breath, too. Everyone took their seats and looked up to the sky. The radio had been turned off, and the bonfires had been left alone for the past hour or so to burn down. Even the area lights had been turned off.

When Hope took her seat, she couldn't stop the grin that spread over her face when Tony sat in the chair next to her. Chills went down her arms, even though she wasn't cold. While the breeze coming in was chilly, her dancing and the warmth from the fires was enough to keep her from putting the blanket she had brought around her shoulders. Maybe later, if it was cold enough, she and Tony could share it.

And when Tony looked at her the way he did, Hope couldn't help but think he might be feeling the bond they were forming too. His hand reached over and took hers. A voice told her it was too soon, but another one was louder and said that she should enjoy this time with him.

When Hope squeezed his hand in return, Tony's eyes sparkled. They continued to stare at one another until the first pop sounded.

Tony winced and closed his eyes.

A loud bang erupted, and the sky filled with light from the first foray of fireworks.

Hope frowned and was about to ask Tony if he was alright, but then he wrenched his hand from hers and jumped up. He pulled her up from the chair and threw her to ground and jumped on top of her.

"Close your eyes, look away from the light. Everything's going to be fine." Tony's hard voice sent chills crawling down Hope's skin.

One moment the man was holding her down, the next, he was being yanked off of her. Then someone pulled her up and to the side.

"Tony? Tony? Are you alright? What happened?" Hope tried to get out of the hands holding her back, but they were too strong for her.

Tony was held tight against Jerod's chest while Megan Anderson, the ranch counselor, and her boyfriend, Daniel Caruthers the foreman over at the Big Sky Christmas Tree Farm, worked to calm Tony down. They also were edging him toward the truck.

"What happened? Is Tony alright?" Nothing seemed alright to Hope. She had no idea what had just happened, and all she could think about was Tony.

"He'll be fine. Don't worry about him. I'm more worried about you." Mike Blankenship's voice was low, but loud enough for her to hear.

Once Tony was out of her sight, Hope looked around and noticed that everyone was looking at her and not at the night sky as it lit up with all of the colors of the American flag. She sighed and relaxed, then looked to see who was holding her back. "Mike, Sam. I'm fine. You can let me go now."

"Are you sure?" Sam was looking at her forehead. "You're bleeding."

Hope put a hand to her head and winced with the pain. "Ouch. What just happened?"

"Come on, let's get your head looked at, and away from all the gossips. Then I'll explain it." Sam led her away, and Rogue followed him without a word. Mike and Nelly also went with them.

Nelly held Buffy's leash, but the dog seemed to be looking for someone. Maybe she wanted to see if Tony was alright? That's exactly what Hope wanted to know too.

<h1 style="text-align:center">Chapter 12</h1>

Tony couldn't believe he had just taken Hope's hand in his. What was he thinking? For a split second he considered letting go, but then her warmth seeped into his palm and then up his arm. There was no way he was letting go now.

Then, when Hope squeezed his hand, a feeling he wasn't accustomed to spread all through his chest. He had to take a few deep breaths in order to keep his breathing normal. Even though the fireworks display was about to begin, he couldn't take his eyes off the beautiful woman sitting next to him and letting him hold her hand.

The thought of kissing her began to take shape in his mind, until a loud bang sounded and he was yanked back to Iraq. He could see the suicide bomber plain as day, standing there in the doorway to the internet café. The Kurdish women were behind him, trying to get out.

Another loud sound exploded around the café, and he knew that the terrorist in front of him was about to let go of his dead man's switch. He had to protect the women. It wasn't just his duty to protect the innocent, it was ingrained in his DNA to protect women and children.

Tony turned to his right to get to the woman closest to him. If he could block the worst of the explosion, he'd wake up in Heaven with God, and those women just might survive. He tackled the closest one, who seemed familiar to him somehow. She must be one of the women he'd been teaching for a few weeks now.

"Close your eyes, look away from the light. Everything's going to be fine." All Tony could do at this point was console the poor woman. She wasn't crying or yelling, she just looked at him in horror with her beautiful green eyes. As he was desperately trying to remember who she was, he expected the bomb to go off. But it didn't. Instead, there was a loud bang, again, and brilliant lights surrounded him. Then he was floating in the sky.

Someone was telling him it was alright. Did he die? Was he on his way to Heaven now? Was St. Peter at the gates waiting to greet him? "Please, save those women. They don't deserve to die at the hands of a terrorist."

"Snap out of it, Tony. You're in Montana, not Iraq. There's no suicide bomber, only fireworks." The woman's voice was calm and collected.

He knew that voice. It was normal, familiar. He could feel his heart racing and his palms were sweating. This wasn't the afterlife. He was still alive. "Megan?"

"Yes, it's me. You're alright. Everyone is alright." Megan smoothed his hair back from his forehead but stayed away from the sensitive areas of his face.

"What happened? What did I just do?" Sense was beginning to return, and Tony could tell from the looks of the people around him that he'd done something to scare them. "Please tell me I didn't hurt anyone."

Tony had heard many stories about how wounded veterans came home with PTSD. Something would set them off, and they'd enter a sort of fugue state where they believed they were back in the sandpit and fighting the enemy. Unfortunately, it also meant they would usually injure someone they loved, or themselves, in the process.

"No one was hurt. You heard the fireworks and it set you off, that's all. We're almost back at the ranch. We can talk about it there, if you like." Megan sat next to him in the ranch van while Jerod drove.

There were also a few other people next to Tony. He looked around and remembered that he'd been sitting with Hope and holding her hand before the chaos had erupted. "Oh, fuuu…fudge nuggets!" Tony had been working on cleaning up his bad language. Most of the time it was no longer an issue, but with the stress of the evening, and what he'd done, looming over him, well, old habits die hard.

Tony dropped his head in his hands. "Did I hurt Hope? Please tell me she's alright." Images of throwing her to the ground floated through his mind, and the memory of what he'd actually done began to replace the memory of the explosion in Iraq. To say he felt terrible was a gross understatement. "She'll probably never want to talk to me again, will she?" This was exactly why he could never have a wife, or even a girlfriend. Even if someone could get past his grotesque scars, he wasn't safe to be around.

Tony was the real-world version of the Beast.

Megan took his hands in hers and in a soft voice conveyed the reality of the situation. "Hope is fine. She was a little surprised, but her first words were for you. She wanted to know if you were alright."

"Pft, yeah right. She probably wanted to know how crazy I really am." Sarcasm dripped from Tony's voice. Then he thought about all the people who'd seen him and hung head his head. "I can never show my face in town again, can I?"

"Captain, you know as well as I do that's not true. This town loves us, and they love their military. You might get some people showing sympathy for you, but you won't get anyone disrespecting you." Jerod kept his eyes on the road, but a few times he looked back through the rearview mirror and was able to make eye contact with Tony.

"Has anyone ever done something as stupid as what I just did?" There was no way Tony was going back to town any time soon. He doubted anyone else had done something like that, and in front of a group of townies, too.

"Actually, yes. One of our guys had a tough time over Christmas when the power went out at the Christmas tree farm. There was a loud popping sound, then the lights went out and people began screaming. His PTSD kicked in, and he had tough time of it until Megan found him." While Jerod would tell the story, he didn't seem willing to share the soldier's name.

But Tony figured that was a good thing. The last person any of them needed gossiping was Jerod. However, maybe this man Jerod was speaking of could help him get through the public embarrassment. Megan could help him deal with his PTSD.

Although, since when did loud noises bother Tony? He'd always loved fireworks and the loud bang they made when the missiles left their silos. As a kid, he and his best buddies would pretend they were actual missiles, sending volleys back to the imaginary enemy after attacking their position.

As far back as Tony could remember, he'd wanted to serve in the Army. That was why he'd joined straight out of college. Even his uncle understood Tony's desire to serve his country and defend their freedom. 9/11 had changed their lives forever. If not for a missed flight, his uncle would have been in the Twin Towers on that fateful day. The Lord was looking out for his family.

After that day, no one questioned Tony's desire to serve his country. The only thing his uncle asked was that he first get his degree, and he did. Which was how Tony was able to rise to the rank of captain before getting blown up by a crazy man who didn't think women should be literate.

But he wasn't a kid anymore. Tony could no longer pretend anything. Life was real, and the fact that he couldn't handle fireworks was real. He should have known he wouldn't handle it well, at least not yet, when he jumped after a car backfired earlier that week. But he hadn't freaked out, just jumped and regurgitated a slew of bad words as his heart hammered against his ribs.

If he hadn't reacted that badly to a car backfiring, why did he go off the rails with fireworks? If anything, he should be getting better with loud noises, not worse. Right? "Megan, why do you think I reacted the way I did? I've never done anything like that before."

The counselor tilted her head. "Do you want to talk about it here, in front of those in the van? Or would you prefer to wait until we're back in my office?"

Tony hadn't even considered those listening in. They were all ranch residents, or workers, so they knew who he was, and they knew what he'd just done. But they didn't have the details on him and his psychological issues. Obviously, Tony didn't know everything about himself, either. "Your office would be good."

Once they were back in Megan's office, just the two of them, Tony took a seat in one of the comfortable microfiber chairs in front of Megan's desk. "You have an idea of why I reacted that way, don't you." It wasn't a question.

Megan tented her fingers in front of her face and sighed. "Why do you think you had such a strong reaction to the loud bang of the fireworks?"

"Argh!" Tony hated the way shrinks always turned the question back on him. If he knew why he had done it, he wouldn't have asked her in the first place. "I don't know." The frustration of the night laced his words and they came out sharper than he intended.

"I know it would be easier if I gave you all the answers, but I can't." Megan pursed her lips, and her own frustration started to show in her posture when she pulled her shoulders back and narrowed her eyes.

"Why can't you? Isn't it your job to know these things?" Now Tony was being combative. But he had earned the right to push back. Tony had been attacked for doing something good; Megan couldn't possibly understand him and what he'd been through.

There was a pregnant pause as Megan looked at Tony, really looked at him. "Are you truly ready to learn the truth?"

"Of course, I am." Tony chuffed. "No matter how painful it is, I *need* to know the truth." He slapped his fist against his chest. "What's that saying? The truth will set you free."

"The truth also hurts." Megan sighed and pursed her lips. She wasn't sure if Tony was ready for this or not, but sometimes you just had to jump and see where you landed.

She sat back in her chair and softened the hard lines on her face. "Tony, you feel safe here at the ranch, right?"

He nodded. "Of course. This is a good place."

"Yes, well." Megan ran her fingernail under her lower lip. She worried the ranch wouldn't feel as safe as he thought it was. "When a soldier is in battle, even after a horrific fight, their brains are hardwired to push the tough emotions to the side."

"Wait, that's not true." Tony had been in several firefights, and he felt the emotions, the pain, the agony of what he had to do. His brain didn't push anything to the side.

Megan held her hands up. "Just wait. Let me finish."

He motioned for her to proceed.

"After decades of psychological research of soldiers in the field, the scientific community all agree that what the person feels during battle may vary depending on the person. There are many reasons behind it, but every one of them do feel some of the fear and loathing that goes along with war. It's natural. If anyone walked away from a battle pumped and happy, ready to go kill more people, then a psychologist would worry about them."

Tony blinked and thought back to his battles. There was one guy who always seemed so excited after battle. Everyone thought he was strange. Turned out he wasn't handling it well at all. He had ignored his emotions and ended up stepping in front of a terrorist with a machine gun. He didn't fight back, didn't scream, he just said, "It's about time."

"You know what I'm talking about, right?" Megan asked.

"Sadly, I do. So, what? We feel part of the emotions if we handle war normally, but not all of it?" While Tony had felt a lot on the battlefield, he was starting to wonder if there wasn't more to it then he'd originally thought. The idea that he didn't suffer from PTSD had gnawed at him, but he hoped he was one of the lucky ones.

"Yes, in essence." Hoping he was beginning to get it, Megan let it sink in before continuing. "Tony." She took a deep breath. "What you have felt since getting out of the Army is a lot of confusion and you've questioned what you will be doing next, right?"

"I was supposed to take over the family business when my uncle retired, but now?" Pain flashed across Tony's face, and he winced. "I don't think my uncle wants to give his business over to a beast." He pointed to his face.

Megan shook her head. "Tony, you are not a beast. You are a handsome man who is talented, smart, and has an easy time making friends. Your uncle is just scared at the moment. If you really want to work in finance, it will happen. I highly doubt that anything you set your mind to won't happen."

The cowboy shrugged and looked down at his hands. "Maybe. But what about tonight?"

The counselor ran a hand over her face and decided to get to the meat of the matter. "Now that you are finally beginning to feel safe, secure, and welcomed, your mind is beginning to unravel…"

"Hold up, my mind is not unraveling!" Tony jumped from his seat and pointed a finger at Megan. He scowled, nostrils flaring.

The demonstration of Tony's anger and fear didn't faze Megan one bit. She'd seen similar actions before, and this wouldn't be the last time one of her patients burst out into a fit. "Tony, please sit down." She pointed to his chair.

When his shoulders sagged, and he let out a long, deep breath, realizing what he had done. He fell back into his chair. "I'm sorry, Megan. I didn't mean to get angry at you. Maybe I am unraveling." He ran a hand through his hair and then shook his head. He wasn't the type to get angry at women, and he certainly wasn't the type to get so aggressive, either.

"Tony, I'm not going to say it's alright, because that sort of outburst isn't alright. But I can say that it's indicative of what you're going through now. Let me finish my explanation before you say anything else, alright?"

Tony looked up into her eyes. He'd trusted this woman with his psychological health so far. "Alright."

"As I was saying, now that your brain is coming to the realization that life is safe, and you have a future, it is beginning to tear away at the walls it built. When you were in battle, your mind had to put up walls to help protect you. It's an automatic fight or flight response. It's completely normal, and expected, of our men and women who see battle. It's also something that happens to women who are in abusive relationships."

War and abuse weren't really the same thing, were they? At least Tony didn't see the connection. But maybe it had something to do with how the brain reacted to intense emotional strain? That he could understand.

"Before now, loud noises were blocked by the walls your mind had constructed. However, now, you don't need them like you once did. So, your brain is working double-time to take those walls down and heal itself from the trauma of war." Megan focused on Tony and leaned forward, putting her arms on her desk. "Does that make sense?"

He took a few seconds to think about it. "So, my brain put up walls so if I heard a loud noise like say a firefight in the distance, or a bomb going off on the other side of camp, I wouldn't freak out and try to hide instead of fighting back?"

A small smile spread across Megan's face. "That's exactly it. And now that your mind and body know you are in a safe place, it wants to deal with the pain and sorrow so that you can fully heal and move forward. But in order to do that, you're going to have to feel everything that those walls kept out."

"There are more tough emotions coming my way? Seriously?" Tony felt the pangs of tears beginning to well in his eyes, and his nose burned. This was too much. He'd already been through so much. It wasn't fair.

"Right now," Megan interrupted his thoughts, "you're probably thinking this isn't very fair. You fought hard for your country, gave up ten years of your life to serve those who stayed behind and protect them from the ravages of terrorists as much as possible."

He nodded.

"But life isn't fair. I know that's harsh, but it's the truth." When Megan paused to take a drink of her water, Tony put his head in his hands.

Megan recognized that he'd had enough for one night and told Tony as much. They could continue to slowly peel back the layers of the walls like an onion. It didn't have to come off like a Band-Aid.

Chapter 13

Hope was a mess.

Not only were her clothes dirty from being thrown to the ground and tackled, but her mind was also disheveled. She needed to know how Tony was doing. One thing Hope knew was that Dana was right: Tony wasn't ready for a relationship. He still needed a lot of counseling.

But he could use a friend. As could she. So the next day after doing her chores, she decided to head over to the ranch and check in on her new friend.

But first, Hope needed to take a trip into town.

The moment Hope walked through the doors of the Frenchtown Roasting Company, she sighed. The scent was heavenly. It wasn't that she was a coffee snob, but her aunt and uncle only brewed that stuff they bought in the grocery store. And it was weak.

Now Lottie, she knew how to roast a great bean and make it strong when she brewed a pot. With notes of cinnamon, chocolate, and some spice she couldn't quite name, Hope was certain a new brew was in the pot that morning—and she wanted to try it.

"Hi, Hope. How goes it?" Dana met her with a cheery greeting.

"Hiya. What's that wonderful scent?" With eyes partway closed, Hope sniffed and a grin spread across her face. Just the scent alone was enough to make her feel better about everything that had happened the day before.

"I'm glad you asked." Lottie walked out from the back of the store with a large pot of something. "This is my latest creation—Panama cinnamon roll blend."

"Wow, that's a mouthful." Hope walked up to the counter, surprised that there wasn't a line at the moment. She looked around. "Where is everyone?"

"Working. The day after a large event, most people are hard at work. We won't see too many ranchers or farmers coming in today. Early this morning, we had a rush from the tourists who left, but now…" Lottie shrugged.

"It's a day to get caught up," Dana added. "We'll do some heavy cleaning this afternoon, once the town folk do their two o'clock pick me up. And then we'll be ready for the rush tomorrow morning."

Even though it was more information that Hope needed, it was actually nice to know. She'd have to make sure to come in the day after a big event whenever she could. "Well, how about a big mug of that new blend, and a coffee cake?"

"Sounds good." Dana rung up her order and served her. Then the two of them sat down to discuss life.

"So, what was the deal with yesterday and Tony?" Hope bit her lower lip, knowing that Dana probably wouldn't be able to say much, but she'd try for whatever information she could get.

"Tony is going to be fine." Dana winced. She knew Hope wanted more than that, but there was no way she was going to say anything else. Patient confidentiality was a huge deal to Jerod.

After taking a sip of her coffee, which was sweeter than she expected, Hope looked at her cousin. "Is there anything you can say?"

Dana shook her head.

"Alright, I'm going out there to visit him myself. I need to see with my own two eyes how he's really doing. I'll be honest, I didn't sleep well last night."

"Hope, I don't know if today is the best time to see him." Dana frowned, then jumped up with a smile. "But, you might have a better chance if you bring treats."

"What kind of treats?" Hope asked.

"Cinnamon rolls, of course." Dana laughed.

"Of course. I should have known. Lottie's cinnamon rolls are probably the biggest hit at the ranch." Even though Hope didn't know the guys all that long, she had seen plenty of them eating Lottie's rolls at the coffee shop, and she'd also seen the boxes at the ranch studded with the sticky remains. One time, she'd even caught Skeeter licking the inside of the box, trying to get every bit of sweet, cinnamon goodness out of it.

So, when Hope walked up to the front door, with a large box of cinnamon rolls inside, she thought for sure she'd be welcome.

It was Jerod who answered the door with drooping eyes. "Hope, I'm sorry but Dana's not here."

"I know, I just saw her at the coffee shop." She held up the box of warm cinnamon rolls, hoping to entice Jerod to open the door for her. "I brought these for everyone."

Instead of the open door as she expected, Jerod walked outside to join her on the porch and closed the door behind him. "I'm sorry you came all the way out here, and brought treats. That was really nice of you. But—" He ran a hand through his hair and looked back at the front window from over his shoulder. "I think it best if you don't come around for a while."

Was she now unwelcomed? Jerod and Dana were family. What in tarnation could she have done that was so awful her own family no longer wanted her around? "What'd I do?"

"Oh." Jerod's face fell, along with his shoulders. "I'm sorry, Hope. You didn't do anything. It's just, well." He let out a long, deep sigh. "I can't say much, but I think it would be best for Tony if you didn't come around for a while."

Hope deflated and almost dropped the box of cinnamon rolls.

Jerod noticed and took them from her, putting them on the table next to the sofa they had on the front porch. "Why don't you sit down." He guided her to the seat.

"Is he alright?" Hope didn't think he'd hurt himself, so the only thing she could think of was he'd had a breakdown of some sort. "How can I help?"

A long moment passed between them before Jerod finally answered, "He's not in a good mental state right now. He said he doesn't want to see you for a while."

Those words hit Hope like a knife through the heart. "I only wanted to be his friend."

"I know. And I'm so sorry. This really has nothing to do with you, exactly. I think he wants to stay clear of all single women for the time being." While it wasn't exactly what Tony had said, Jerod inferred that from what the cowboy *did* say that morning. "Give him some time. PTSD doesn't always begin right away. Sometimes, it can come on slowly over time, or years down the road one thing can happen and then, bam! It hits a soldier like a ton of bricks."

Hope's eyes widened, and her pulse quickened. She'd never seen a PTSD attack before. She'd heard about them, even seen something on TV once, but it wasn't anything like what the media portrayed. "You think my being near him is the inciting event?"

Jerod shook his head and waved his hands in front of him. "No. That's not what I was saying. It was the fireworks." He began to pace the front porch. "Did Dana tell you about my issues with PTSD?"

A frown slowly spread across Hope's face. "No, I don't think so." Hope and Dana had spoken, but no details had been shared about Jerod's issues. Just that he had some, and Dana helped him.

He stopped pacing and took a seat on the rocking chair near Hope. "Most servicemembers who have seen combat, or lived through an explosion of some sort, have PTSD in varying degrees. Like Tony, I didn't think mine was too bad, at first."

His nostrils flared and Jerod jumped up from his seat to resume his pacing. "I almost crashed my truck when Dana and I first began dating. A loud sound sent me into a tailspin while I was driving, and if not for her soothing voice, and quick thinking, we would have crashed on a mountain highway."

Fear filled Hope's entire being. Not only for Dana and Jerod, but also for Tony. "Will Tony be safe?"

"Yes." Jerod nodded. "He's not going to be leaving the ranch, or even going off on the ranch by himself for a while."

"I see." Hope didn't really, but she wasn't sure what else to say. It was a lot more serious than she thought it was. "Um, if you think it won't hurt him, tell Tony I said hi and that I'll be praying for him." She stood up to leave and pointed to the box of cinnamon rolls. "Those are for everyone, but you might want to keep Skeeter away until all have had a chance." She smiled and walked to her truck with her head held high.

Hope kept up the pretense of strength until she was out of sight of the ranch and then she pulled over to the side of the road and let the tears fall. An ache so deep she didn't even know where it began took root. All she wanted was to help Tony. If she wasn't allowed to see him, how could she help?

A verse she'd learned years ago, but thought she'd forgotten, came to mind.

Be careful for nothing; but in everything by prayer and supplication with thanksgiving let your requests by made known unto God. And the peace of God, which passeth all understanding, shall keep your hearts and minds through Christ Jesus.

Philippians 4:6-7

God was listening to her. Hope knew that beyond anything else: as long as she looked to God for the answers, then he would give them to her. She dried her tears and took a deep breath. Then she prayed until she had no more to let off her chest.

Hope sat there waiting for a message from God. Part of asking God for help was also listening. It wasn't that she expected the clouds to part and a light to shine down on her. Or a loud voice from Heaven to give her the answers. No, she knew from past experience that the Holy Spirit would most likely give her peace to begin with. Then, when there was something for her to do, the Spirit would lead her down that path. As long as she was listening for the still, small voice, she'd know what to do when the time came.

For now, she needed to get home and back to work. Sometimes, a long, hard day of work would help clear her mind, and while she may not get her answers today, she would definitely find a small measure of peace.

Chapter 14

Tony was dragging as he headed down the hall for breakfast, or what was left of it. He'd had a rough night, full of nightmares, and hadn't been able to get back to sleep. Normally, he'd be up at the crack of dawn to help with the chores around the ranch, but that morning no one bothered him.

Which was a good thing since he hadn't gotten to sleep until well after four in the morning. Five hours of sleep wasn't ideal, but with coffee and some eggs, he'd do fine.

When he was a few feet away from the kitchen, the sharp scent of coffee hit his nose, and he inhaled deeply. It wasn't until he turned the corner and saw the kitchen counter that he picked up the scent of cinnamon and sugar. A beep came from the microwave, and he almost grinned. Someone must have gone into town for Lottie's famous cinnamon rolls. No one did breakfast like Lottie Hamilton.

"You had better've saved me at least one of those rolls," Tony growled when he noticed two warm rolls sitting on a plate in Skeeter's hand.

The young man grimaced. "Why, Tony, I thought you'd already gotten up and eaten."

"I take it that means you're eating the last two?" Tony arched a brow and glared the man down.

Skeeter pulled at his collar and looked everywhere but at Tony. "I, ah, you can have one of mine."

"Actually," Jerod said loudly as he stalked toward Skeeter. "Both of those are for Tony. I told you, you could only have the one I gave you an hour ago."

Skeeter set the plate down on the counter and skedaddled out the back door before anyone could say anything else.

Jerod chuckled. "Sorry about that. I did try to save them for you. But Skeeter has a way of finding even the tiniest crumb if it came from something Lottie baked."

"So true. Did you see him last week when he was licking the box?" Tony picked up the plate and got himself a fresh fork before getting a cup of coffee to go with his breakfast.

"Yeah, I think the entire house saw it, or at least heard about it." Jerod shook his head. "I swear, if I didn't know better, I'd say he was still only thirteen. I don't know how he made it so long in the Army."

"Probably because the sergeants stayed on his backside every minute of every day. I bet he did the most push-ups in basic and AIT." Tony finished fixing up his coffee and sat at the table to dig into breakfast.

"I'd bet he set a record for the number of push-ups one soldier did the entire time he was in. And the poor guy still had scrawny arms." A deep chuckled escaped Jerod, and he filled up his coffee before joining Tony at the table.

Out of the corner of his eye, Tony watched Jerod looking at his plate. "You better not have any designs on my cinnamon rolls."

Jerod help up his hands in surrender. "Nope, I already had one." He took a sip of coffee. "I was actually trying to figure out a way to bring up who brought us those cinnamon rolls."

With a giant piece on his fork, Tony shoved it into his mouth. After only a couple of chews, he turned his gaze to Jerod. "Who brought them?"

Jerod turned his head away and took another long sip of his hot coffee.

"Jerod. Who was it?" Tony put his fork down and narrowed his eyes at his friend.

"Hope Lowry." Jerod wasn't one to play games, or draw things out. So he blurted the name of the giver.

Tony sat back in his chair and exhaled. "Is Hope alright?"

"She's fine, Tony. The poor cowgirl was worried about you. She wanted me to tell you she was praying for you and she hoped you'd enjoy the cinnamon rolls." Still not wanting to look at Tony, but knowing he needed to gauge the man's well-being, Jerod risked a glance over the rim of his coffee cup.

Pain crossed Tony's face. It was evident that Tony felt awful about what had happened. "Look, man. She's fine," Jerod said quickly. "Hope understands you need time."

Tony dropped his head into his hands. "I don't need time. I'll never be good enough for her. She deserves a man who isn't hideously scarred, or isn't afraid of loud sounds. She's better off with someone else."

"Tony, I think for now, she just wants to be there for you. All she seems to be offering is friendship. Maybe you should think about taking her up on her offer." If it had been any other woman, Jerod wouldn't have believed she was offering only friendship. But Jerod knew enough about Hope to know she wasn't in a position to go out with anyone, either.

Just the night before, Jerod and Dana had talked about the pair. They both agreed that they'd make a great couple, once they dealt with their issues. And until then, it would be good for them both to become friends. The problem was Tony. He most likely wouldn't want to be friends with any single woman for a while. He had too much healing to do.

Over the coming weeks, Tony was scheduled to have daily sessions with Megan as well as his group sessions each week.

It was only one day later in his private session with Megan when he really made a breakthrough.

Tony was on the road to healing; he'd even begun to feel safe again. The Fourth of July fireworks were a distant memory, and he was ready to move forward.

Megan sat across from him this time in one of the stuffed chairs. "When in battle, the mind protects itself from too much negative input. But once you begin to relax and feel safe, the memories—the fears—will begin to work themselves out in a way we may not expect. What happened that night is normal. Now comes the hard part: dealing with the emotions tied to the bombing. Eventually, you will enjoy fireworks again. It may never be the same, and you might flinch when they begin, but you'll get to a point where you won't go back to the internet café in your mind. You'll move past it, you won't ever forget it, but once you forgive—"

"Wait. Forgive? Why? He doesn't deserve it." Tony frowned and fisted his hands in his lap. He didn't want to go off on Megan again. Something inside of him told him to relax and listen to what Megan was telling him. She was the expert, after all.

"Tony, forgiveness is about you, not him. When you forgive someone, it doesn't mean you are saying what they did was alright. It means that you are ready to let go of the pain, and even hatred, and move forward with your own healing." Megan paused as she let it sink in for Tony.

When it was obvious that he had chewed on her words long enough, she changed tact. "But more importantly, it is God who commands us to forgive those who have hurt us." Again, she paused.

"And what if I can't forgive him?" Even though the terrorist had killed himself, which made it impossible for Tony to tell him that he forgave the murderer, he wasn't sure he could let the anger go.

"Then you will have a deep rift between you and God. I'm no preacher, but I do know enough about the Bible to know that there are many versus where Jesus tells us to forgive one another. In fact, Ephesians 4:32 is coming to mind right now. 'And be kind to one another, tenderhearted, forgiving one another, even as God in Christ forgave you.'"

The truth of her words hit Tony hard. He knew she was right, and he needed to work on forgiving the man who had destroyed his world. But that was going to take time.

"Why don't you pray about this, and see how things go? In the meantime, I have something else that might help you." Megan stood up and went around to the other side of her desk.

The something else Megan spoke about turned out to be a pleasant surprise. One he wasn't sure was the right choice for him, but one he was also beginning to come around to – time with Buffy.

The next day, Nelly showed up with the dogs. Spending time with Buffy did seem to smooth out the rough spots for Tony. His anger was subsiding, and he found that he wanted to find a way to forgive.

"Nelly, can a dog really make a big difference for someone battling PTSD?" Tony knew he was back on the battlefield, only this time, he wasn't on a literal field like when he was in Iraq. At times he felt he was in the sandpit fighting to help the locals live a worthy life, as well as protect his men, but this battle was coming from within.

The dog whisperer stood up from where she had been petting Angel. "Actually, yes. You've seen the improvement with Sam, haven't you?"

Sam Marley had been the first veteran at the Crooked Arrow Ranch to be paired with a service dog. Rogue had chosen Sam almost from the beginning. Only no one had really recognized the attachment the dog and human were building, no one except Nelly Wilson.

She worked several days a week at the ranch with the men and her three dogs. She had two more coming soon, but until she paired another soldier with one of her dogs, she couldn't take in any more dogs.

"Yes, but I thought that had more to do with you." Tony grinned at Sam's girlfriend.

It was a rough start, but Sam and Nelly had begun dating not too long after Rogue and Sam were paired up. In fact, Sam was doing so well, he worked part-time for Nelly. And the changes in the man were like night and day.

Nelly didn't blush from his teasing, like he expected, instead she fisted her hands on her hips. "Actually, he began making significant changes the moment Rogue attached himself to Sam." She conveniently left out how much Sam had improved after she had attached herself to him, too.

Tony laughed. "I know, I know. But"—he put a finger in the air—"you've got to admit that having you in his life has contributed to his overall well-being."

She tilted her head and considered his statement. "Yes, I think so. But he has so much more going on in his life than a girlfriend."

"That's right." A deep voice said from Tony. "You aren't by chance teasing my woman, are you?" Sam stepped around Tony and looked him in the eye, daring him to keep it up.

Tony put his hands in the air as though he was surrendering a fight. "No, of course not." He followed that up with a cheese-eating grin.

Rogue stood at attention next to Sam and stared at Tony. The rust-colored boxer was a very gentle dog but also completely loyal to Sam and Nelly. While the dog didn't growl or do anything aggressive, Tony knew that if he stepped out of line, the dog would insert himself between them.

He could respect that. Having a partner that was totally devoted to him would be nice. Tony turned his head and noticed Buffy trotting over. She had been working with Dixon, but the two of them hadn't really hit it off.

Buffy, a chocolate Labrador, loved women. Men? Not so much. However, she had taken a strong liking to Tony. And Tony liked her as well, even though he was adamant that he didn't need a service dog.

Nelly knew that in time, Buffy would work her magic on Tony, and lately, he seemed more open to spending time with the service dog. She'd been trained to help veterans suffering from PTSD, and Nelly had been secretly training her to help Tony with his disability, not hearing on his left side.

In fact, Buffy walked up to Tony's left and nudged his thigh, her way of letting him know she was there. Tony's vision was just fine, it was his hearing that left him wary of anyone nearing him from the left. He would still jerk if someone came up on his left side, oblivious until they were within arm's length of him.

That was exactly what Buffy was for; her job was to notify Tony with a nudge to his left whenever someone was coming toward them on his left side. That way, Tony would realize that there was a potential threat approaching. Most people in their area weren't actual threats, but a wounded vet suffering from PTSD didn't instinctively know that, like someone who had never served.

When Tony felt Buffy next to him, he looked down and patted the dog's head. *"Braver hund."* Nelly had taught him that phrase—good dog—as well as the other German commands for the dogs when they were working.

After Tony smiled at Buffy, she nodded her head and chuffed as though she was telling Tony he was a good human. He liked that. "You know, I heard that we have a female wounded veteran arriving in the next two weeks. Will you be training Buffy for her?"

Not wanting to commit to anything, Nelly smiled and shrugged. "I don't choose the partners; the dogs do the choosing."

It was the same thing, over and over. Nelly always told Tony the dogs did the choosing and then look between Buffy and him. He felt as though she was trying to tell him something, but he was unable to understand. Why did women do that? The never came right out and said what they meant. It was so frustrating.

Tony didn't know a single man who understood women and their cryptic communication. He looked to Sam. "How in the world do you communicate with her?"

Sam grinned. "I just ask her what she means. It took a while, but she's more straightforward with me now."

"Pft. You mean it took you a while to finally listen?" Nelly rolled her eyes heavenward, then bussed a quick peck on Sam's cheek.

A small pang of jealousy hit Tony's heart. If only he could find a woman who would love him for who he was now. Someone who could look past his scars. Before joining the Army, Tony never had a problem catching a woman's eye. But now, the only time they looked at him, it was with horror or pity in their eyes. Well, okay, so maybe Hope had moved past that part.

Tony wasn't sure why he kept thinking about her. Maybe it was because a certain cousin of Hope's was always talking about her? He wasn't sure.

"Hiya. How goes it today?" Dana's chipper greeting jolted Tony from his thoughts.

For the past two weeks, at least three times a week, the wife of the ranch owner had come to him with either a funny story about Hope or a message from her. It seemed he hadn't scared away the pretty maiden, at least not yet. Tony was sure Dana would say something about her cousin, again.

The smile slowly faded from Dana's face as she stared Tony in the eyes. "Um, what's your plans for today?"

The woman's hands began to fidget in front of her, and Tony got a sinking feeling in his gut. "Why?"

Dana bit her lower lip. "Well, I wanted to go riding with Hope today. The horse she rides at home isn't feeling so well."

"What does that have to do with me and my plans?" It wasn't as though Hope would ride his horse, so he couldn't understand how this affected him.

"Well, I thought she could come over here this afternoon and go riding on our land." Dana looked up. "The summer is coming to a close soon, and I was hoping to get in some more late afternoon rides before the cold settles in."

Tony blinked a few times, then looked around him. "I don't think the summer is over yet, it's only the beginning of August."

"I take it this is your first summer in Montana?" Dana grinned.

Tony nodded.

"Well, unless we are going to have an Indian summer, which we aren't, then come the beginning of September, the nights will start to cool down. By the end of the month, we'll be wearing jackets again. It's even possible to get snow before we change the calendars over to October."

"Okay, that's all fine and dandy, but again, what does that have to do with my plans?" Tony still wasn't getting it. Dana could go riding any time she wanted, and she certainly didn't need his permission.

"It's just that I know you don't want to see Hope yet. So if you aren't riding this afternoon, then I'll have Hope drive around to the barn by four o'clock so we can go riding. We shouldn't be gone long, dinner will be ready by six." Dana rushed on, "But don't worry, Hope won't stay."

It still wasn't registering with Tony. While he hadn't seen Hope since the Fourth of July, it wasn't as though she was banned from the ranch. But as he thought about, he finally realized that other than the day after the fireworks, Hope had not set foot on the ranch. At least, not that he'd seen or heard.

"Do you mean to tell me that Hope was banished from the ranch because of me?" Tony couldn't believe it. Incredulity laced his words. If Hope thought he didn't want to see her, then he'd feel like a heel. But where did that idea come from?

Dana looked to Nelly, who took Sam by the arm and led him away. All the dogs, except for Buffy, followed them. "Uh, I thought you knew."

"Is this some sort of female code again? Really, just say it outright because I'm totally confused." In fact, Tony was beginning to get a headache. This round and round thing that women did was senseless.

"I thought you were the one who said you didn't want to see Hope around here?" Dana hadn't heard those words from Tony, but she had heard them from her husband, Jerod. And she thought it was a sentiment that the counselor agreed with.

"The only time I didn't want to see her was on July fifth." He thought about that for a moment and realized he had made a couple of comments to Megan during his private counseling sessions. The only reason he didn't want to see Hope was because he was too embarrassed. He'd tackled her to the ground and acted as though he was saving her from a suicide bomber for Pete's sake. And he'd freaked out in the middle of a bonfire in front of the entire town.

On a holiday, no less.

"So, you didn't want Hope to stay away forever? Just for the one day?" Now it was Dana's turn to be confused.

As Tony remembered some of what he'd said in session, he began to feel uneasy. He put his hands in his front pockets and looked down at the ground. There was a small rock close to his foot. He nudged it away with the pointed toe of his boot. "Well, I might have said a few things to Megan over the past month. But I didn't mean for Hope to be banned from the ranch. She's your family, and as such has every right to come here and visit you."

Dana scrunched her nose. "Sounds like we need to get better at communication. Jerod thought having Hope here would hinder your recovery. Or at least make it very tough to move forward."

Tony shook his head. "That's not true. While, yes, I didn't want to see her those first few days." Then he mumbled under his breath, "And maybe a few more." Then he quickly followed up his foolish statement when he realized Dana had heard him. "I didn't mean for her to stay away so long. Honest. I just thought that I could avoid her if she came by before I was ready to see her again, that's all."

"So, let me get this straight." Dana waited for his reply.

Tony motioned with his hand for Dana to continue.

"You don't have a problem with Hope coming over for a visit?" If that was the case, maybe Hope could stay for dinner, after all. Dana was beginning to mentally make all sorts of plans for her cousin at the ranch.

"No, I don't. She's your family and this is your home. I don't want to get in the way."

"But, would it bother you to see her?" That was the big question Dana had. She had no desire to set him back in the progress he'd made over the past month.

Tony scratched his stubbly chin and thought for a moment. Thoughts of the pretty woman entered his mind, and he remembered how much fun they'd had before the fireworks went off. Then he winced with pain as he remembered, again, what he'd done.

"Never mind. I won't have her over." Dana pursed her lips when she realized she'd caused Tony pain. That was never her intention.

He held his hand up. "No, no. I was thinking about something else. I think it might be good for me to see Hope again." Tony hoped he hadn't hurt her feelings, and he wanted to ask Dana about it, but thought better of it. "Is she... Does she want to see me?"

Dana almost laughed. It was beginning to feel like high school all over again. "Of course she does. How many times a week do I bring you a message from her? She really does want to be your friend, Tony. And I think you could use a friend right now. Someone who isn't going through the same things you are. You have plenty of those types of friends around here." Dana waved to encompass the ranch.

He nodded. "You're right. It might be nice to have a friend who isn't always talking about where she fought, or who she fought, or really, any sort of military reference." He stopped and wondered aloud, "What would be talk about?"

Dana shrugged. "I don't know, normal stuff? Like horses and ranching? The latest movies? Or where you were on 9/11? You know, the stuff everyone talks about who hasn't been in the military."

"Really? You ask people where they were on 9/11?" Tony thought back and realized he had been in high school when it happened.

"I was in junior school. I remember we had a TV in the classroom and someone had checked their phone between classes and their mom had left a message about what happened, so she and asked the teacher. She didn't know so she turned on the TV, I suspect she thought the girl was lying. But all of the channels had been taken over by the news. Nothing else was on, not even the daytime soaps. The rest of the school day nothing was done in any of our classes. Those who had TVs turned them on. And those who didn't, turned on a radio." Dana wiped a tear from her cheek.

"It was similar in my high school. For weeks it was all anyone talked about. That was when I knew I had to join. I already wanted to, but that just reinforced my need to do something." Tony never thought he was a hero, but he had always been a patriot. And he wasn't going to stay home all safe and cozy while good men and women of the US Armed Forces died for him and his family. No, he knew the best way to beat those terrorists and keep his country safe was through numbers. No one could beat the US in military force or numbers. Well, maybe China could beat the US in numbers, but not force.

"Yeah, a lot of the guys I graduated high school with joined right after graduating. It was scary." Dana shivered as she recalled the guy she had crushed on for a while. Adam joined up, but he never made it home. He wasn't the only one, either.

"You know, my grandfather used to talk about where he was when JFK was shot. Do you think it's normal for everyone to talk about where they were and what they remembered when some major event happened?" Tony had never realized it, but he and his buddies had talked about 9/11 as well. He just assumed that since they'd all joined the Army, it was normal for them. He never thought civilians talked about it too.

"Actually, I remember my mom talking about the space shuttle blowing up. One night my parents had a few new friends over and they all sat around talking about that event. It's part of the history books now, so we discussed it in school, but not like the way my parents did." Dana tilted her head. "How strange."

"Where was Hope on 9/11?" Now Tony was curious. It wasn't something he'd ever considered asking her.

A grin spread from ear to ear on Dana's face. "You'll have to ask her the next time you two speak."

Chapter 15

"Are you sure? Jerod won't be mad at you, or me?" Hope worried at her lower lip and prayed neither of them would get in trouble. The last thing she wanted was to be the cause of a rift between Dana and Jerod.

Dana's stern voice came over the phone loud and clear. "Come on, already. Get over here. And don't worry. Tony told me himself that he'd like to see you again."

Hope's eyes brightened at the thought of seeing her cowboy again. Then she stopped short. Where did that thought come from? He wasn't *her* cowboy. They were barely friends. More like acquaintances than anything else. And besides, she still wasn't in the right frame of mind to go out with anyone.

No, friendship was all she had to offer anyone, no matter how good they looked in cowboy boots and a Stetson. She grabbed her keys, purse, and headed out.

The drive to the ranch was too long, but at the same time, too short.

The butterflies that had fluttered in Hope's gut quickly turned into a buzzing so hard and fast that she had to categorize them as bees by the time she parked her truck at the Crooked Arrow Ranch. Part of her hoped that she *wouldn't* see Tony. But then she chastised herself for that thought and prayed God would give her the strength to be a good friend to the man.

Hope opened the door to her old, beat-up, blue Ford F150 pickup and stepped out. The poor thing had seen better days, but she wasn't going to get rid of it any time soon. As long as it still got her from point A to point B safely, she'd keep it. Ratty old seats and all.

When she took a breath, her nose itched, and her throat burned. "Fire?" She looked around but couldn't see any smoke. So she walked up to the front door and knocked.

Dana answered the moment Hope pulled her hand back. The woman must have been waiting on the other side of the door for her. "Come in." The sour look on her face was enough to douse any excitement Hope might have had about this visit.

"What's going on?" Hope looked around but didn't see anyone else in the entryway.

"Fire season. That's what." Dana pulled her cousin into the kitchen where she had two tall glasses of sweet tea waiting for them, along with a cheese platter.

Hope eyed the treats and frowned. "I thought we were going for a ride?"

"So did I. Until Jerod smelled the smoke." Dana's brow furrowed. "Didn't you smell it?"

"Yeah." Hope nodded. "I did, but I didn't see any smoke. How far away is it?"

"Far enough that we don't have to worry, yet. But Jerod doesn't want us out riding in this. In fact, he and the guys are out right now bringing in the cattle so nothing is out in the open. He doesn't want to have to worry about tracking down any of our animals should the winds change course and bring fire our way." Dana turned worried eyes out the back of the house and looked for her husband.

"How long have they been gone?" Hope had seen her fair share of wildfires. She'd never lost a building, but there had been a few head of cattle lost to smoke inhalation one summer.

Dana sucked her lips in her mouth and looked at her watch. "Two hours."

"Why didn't you call me? I could have come over sooner and helped." Hope began pacing in the kitchen. "I wonder if your parents know?"

"Did you see them before leaving?" Dana turned her attention back to her cousin, now worrying about her parents and their farm.

Hope shook her head. "No. I saw them this morning and told them where I'd be this afternoon. But I haven't seen them since breakfast." She pulled her cell phone out of her purse and noticed two missed text messages and a voicemail from her uncle. She held her phone out for Dana to see.

"Oh no. I hope they're alright." Dana put a hand to her mouth.

"I'm sure they're fine. Do you know where the fire is?" The farm where Hope was now living was to the southeast of the Crooked Arrow. If the fire was to the north, then the Baker Farm was in no danger.

Dana nodded. "Yeah, it's coming from Idaho, straight to the west and just a bit north."

Relief flooded into Hope. "Then we should be safe for a long while yet. The firefighters will get it out before it even gets close to us. Do you know if the ranch has prepared for the season yet? Do they have at least a five-foot safety zone between their land and the neighbors'?" Even with five feet of nothing but dirt, fire could get into their land and spread through the dry grass. But it would take a big gust of wind to do so.

"I don't know. Maybe they're clearing paths now? They've been gone too long to just be bringing in our small herd." The ranch didn't have a lot of land, or a lot of animals, but they did keep some cattle and sheep. More to provide them with the meat they needed throughout the year and enough to use to teach the wounded vets how to work a ranch. They even bought and sold their cattle on the local market as a teaching tool.

"Maybe they're out checking the fence lines, making sure there's nothing that could help the fire move through your land?" Hope had done her fair share of riding fence lines looking for anything, besides the fence itself, that might burn and allow the fire to pass through to hers or her neighbor's land.

Dana nodded. "Maybe. I think I should try calling Jerod just to see." She pulled out her cell phone. Instead of reaching him, it went straight to voicemail. "Ugh, I hate that we don't have good cell coverage out here."

"Did he bring a radio?" Hope asked, looking around to see if she could find a radio charging station. There were three spots open, meaning someone had taken three radios out. "Looks like he took them."

"Oh, thanks." Dana chuckled. "I think I'm a bit scatter-brained at the moment. Too much worry."

They both walked to the station, and Dana took the remaining radio off the charger and called for anyone to answer. "Hello? Anyone got a radio?" Worry lines etched around Dana's eyes as she looked from the radio to her cousin.

Not wanting to let Dana handle it all on her own, Hope reached out and took the radio from her cousin. "Let me try. Jerod? Tony? Anyone receiving?"

A crackle came over the radio and what sounded like someone trying to respond, but neither of them could make it out, or who it was attempting to converse with them.

"Say again? You're breaking up." Hope put the radio to her ear in an effort to hear better, knowing full well it wouldn't help. If they were out of range, then she wouldn't receive them, and they wouldn't receive her, either.

Another crackle, this time shorter, came through and then nothing but dead air.

With a sigh, Hope put the radio back on the charger. "I think they're too far out. You might want to have Jerod get a repeater set up so you can hear each other from anywhere on your property."

Dana scrubbed her face and wrung her hands together. "We do. So, either something is wrong, or they're no longer on our property."

Things weren't looking good, but Hope wasn't going to jump to conclusions, not yet. "Let's go with they're out there helping a neighbor. Who knows, maybe a neighbor's cow broke down the fence and they decided to take the cow back?"

"Pft, yeah right." Dana shook her head.

"Okay, so that might not be it, but I wouldn't put it past Jerod and the guys to go help your neighbors. Why don't we make some more tea and stay here? We can man the radio and every so often check to see if they're back in range." From past experience, Hope knew the best thing they could do was keep cool and stay at the house. Someone needed to man the radio, just in case.

And besides, she knew Jerod well enough to know that he wouldn't want his new wife out in this weather. Even if the fire never got close enough to pose a danger, they should stay at the house. Jerod would look there first when he returned.

A few different emotions flittered across Dana's face. Hope understood her cousin enough to know that she was considering the odds that Jerod was just being neighborly to someone. "You're probably right. He's always trying to help others."

Hope guided her cousin back to the kitchen and had her sit at the counter while she went about preparing a snack. Nothing worked better than a little chocolate. And while Hope didn't know this kitchen well, she knew her cousin well enough to know where she kept the contraband. With a house full of men, Dana had to have hidey-hole of some sort to keep her sweets safe.

In the back of the pantry, Hope found exactly what she was looking for. Hope pulled the tin can out and opened it up to discover what looked like a container of veggie crisps was actually a baggie full of salted caramels. The good kind too.

When she brought it over to where Dana sat, her cousin took one out of the tin without even looking and began nibbling on it. Hope joined her and sighed. "This is the good stuff. I don't know how you've kept these away from Skeeter, but boy am I glad you did."

"Hm?" Dana looked to her cousin. "Oh, yes. Skeeter." A sly smile crossed her face. "I bought the tin full of veggie crisps. When I tried to share them with the guys, they all scrunched their noses and looked away, like a dog realizing that the treat you were about to give him had a pill inside it." She chuckled.

"Good job. Now you know how to hide the good stuff." Hope plopped the rest of her treat in her mouth and slowly chewed, doing her best to keep from moaning. She hadn't had any of the expensive ooey gooey treats since last Christmas.

"Actually, Skeeter tried them." Dana snorted with the memory. "Then he did just like a dog and spit it out. He was about to just throw it on the table, but I glared at him and growled under my breath. Immediately, he stood up and went to the trash can and threw it out. Then I called out for him to wash his hands."

Hope joined in the laughter, knowing that Dana needed it. "I can totally picture it too. Skeeter's a nice guy, I really do like him, but..."

"But he needs to grow up. I know." Dana sighed. "Lord knows that I'm trying. Maybe one day he'll meet a nice, young lady who won't accept his behavior and then he'll be forced to grow up?" She raised her brows at the idea.

Hope shrugged. "Maybe." Then she took another large square and began nibbling. "These are sooo good. But, you know, if the guys come back and see this tin out, they'll know your secret."

Dana picked up the tin, pulled out a few more pieces, and set them on the counter. Then she closed it up and put it away. "That's why I always take a few out and put the tin back. That way, if anyone catches me eating these, they won't know where to look."

"Oh, you are too devious. I love it." Hope picked up the pieces on the counter and put them on a napkin. Then they both went to sit at the kitchen table while they waited.

While the salted caramel chocolates satisfied their sweet toothes, it didn't fill their bellies. "How about I fix up some soup and sandwiches? Maybe tomato soup and grilled cheese? We can hold off on grilling their sandwiches until we see them." Hope knew Dana needed something to do in order to keep her mind off of the sad possibilities. Even though it was most likely that everyone was helping out the neighbors, it was much easier to immediately go to the worst-case scenario.

Dana put a hand over Hope's. "What do you say we pray first? Ask God to protect everyone."

Feeling like a fool for not thinking of that herself, Hope's shoulders drooped. "Of course. We should have done that first thing. I'm sorry I didn't think of it."

"I didn't think of it, either. It took getting some sugar and chocolate in my system to start thinking straight." Dana chuckled and went to get her Bible.

They both sat holding hands at the dining room table while Dana started out the prayer. "Lord, I humbly come to you and ask that you put a hedge of protection around my husband and the rest who are with him. You know where they are and what they are doing, please sustain them and keep them safe, Lord. And I ask that you help the firefighters who are working to stop this forest fire from getting any larger. Keep them safe, and help their loved ones to not worry like we've been doing. I give you my worry and fears and trust that you will do what's best."

Hope picked up the prayer when she realized Dana had paused. "Father, thank you that the fire isn't too close to us. I also ask that you protect the firefighters, and anyone who is in the way of the fires. Also, please help the wildlife to escape the fire as well as the smoke. And I want to echo what Dana said, please keep Jerod and all the men safe. Bring them home unharmed, Lord. In Jesus's name I pray, amen."

She knew that long drawn-out prayers weren't needed. A simple request was all God wanted from his children. God knew best how to handle these situations, all she and Dana needed to do was ask for their heart's desire and thank God for taking such great care of them. It truly was a blessing that the fire wasn't too close.

"How about some soup now?" Hope stood and went to get the large cans of tomato soup she had seen in the cabinet earlier.

"I think that sounds great. I'll prepare the cheese sandwiches for grilling." This was exactly what Dana needed, a job. Something to keep her hands moving and her mind off of Jerod.

Once the soup was on the stove, Hope called her aunt and uncle and left them a voicemail telling them what was happening and that she was going to stay with Dana until Jerod returned. She also asked that they call her and let her know they were alright.

"Voicemail? Where do you think they are?" Now Dana had turned her worry to her parents.

Maybe Hope should have made that call far enough away that Dana couldn't have heard her. "I think they're feeding the stock." Hope looked at the clock. "It's about time for dinner in the barn." She grinned at her cousin and lightly pushed her shoulder. "Remember?"

When Dana's brow puckered with confusion, Hope reminded her. "When we were like, oh, I don't know? Ten or eleven?" She put a finger to her chin, then nodded. "I think we were eleven. Anyway, remember that summer when we tried to feed our vegetables to the horses?"

Realization dawned on Dana's face. "That's right! I totally forgot. Snickers, my horse at the time, turned his nose up and snickered as though he knew exactly what we were up to and he wasn't about to get involved."

"And when your mom saw us, she asked why we were trying to have dinner in the barn." Hope laughed.

"Then she made us a new plate of vegetables and sat with us until we finished it all." Dana stuck her tongue out. "I still don't like very many vegetables to this day. I swear it's because of that night." She shivered. "Cold, soggy vegetables? Gross."

"I know, right? I still can't look at brussels sprouts without my stomach getting queasy. I've even tried them baked with cheese and bacon. Still no way, no how for me." Hope put a hand to her stomach shook her head.

"I can eat asparagus now, but only if it's grilled right. It can't be soggy, or cold. They must be warm with olive oil, garlic, and a few other spices. Bacon crumbles sure help too." Dana gave her cousin a conspiratorial look. "We should make some veggies for the men when they get back. You know, as a thank you for the hard work they did today."

"Don't you mean as a punishment for not checking in?" Hope put her hands on her hips and shook her head.

Both women were laughing when a voice sounded over the radio. "Dana? Can you hear me?"

"It's Jerod!" Dana screamed as she jumped up and ran to the bank of radios. "Jerod! Where are you? Are you safe? What happened?" She let off a string of more questions, not letting up on the radio button long enough for Jerod to explain.

"Dana, let him talk now." Hope took the radio out of her cousin's hand and held it away so the man could speak.

A hearty chuckle could be heard over the radio waves. "Thanks, Hope. I was wondering when she'd let me talk. We're all safe. Are you?" He let his button go.

Hope depressed the talk button on the radio and let him know they were safe, just worried about him and the others.

"I'll explain when we get in, just know that we are all safe. Stinky, but safe." Jerod's laugh could be heard as he pulled the radio away from his face and then let the button go.

Dana pulled the radio from Hope's hand. "Jerod, honey, when will you be back?"

"We should be at the barn in the next twenty minutes or so. And I should warn you, everyone is starving. Skeeter even said he'd eat those veggie crisps of yours if there were any left, he's that hungry."

Dana and Hope exchanged a worried glance.

"We have tomato soup on the stove, and I'll have grilled cheese sandwiches ready for everyone when you get here. No need for vegetables." Dana wasn't about to let the young cowboy find out where she kept her stash. She'd grill him up a steak if need be, just to keep the man out of her salted caramels.

Chapter 16

Tony was dripping with sweat and covered in soot, dirt, and Lord only knew what else. But he was so happy to see the top of the barn when they crested the small hill that he didn't care how dirty, or stinky, he was. All he wanted was a large glass of cold sweet tea and some of that food he heard Dana telling Jerod about.

When they entered the house through the back door, Dana and Hope stood to the side with a tray full of tall, cold water.

"Here, drink this up. I'm sure y'all need water first." Dana handed Jerod a glass.

Hope held out a glass and was happy to see a smile on Tony's face when he took her offering.

The rest of the men all took a glass, and when everyone had downed their water, they began talking all at once.

"Okay, okay." Dana laughed, excited to see everyone had made it home safely. "I've got food on the table, but if you want to clean up first…"

"Oh, heck no!" Skeeter called out. "I want one of those sandwiches you promised, maybe even two or three." He covered his stomach with his hand and shoved his way through the throng of men blocking his path to the kitchen.

While all the men jockeyed for position at the table, Tony watched and smiled. He was so glad to be home. But he was also proud of what they'd done that day.

"What's the smile for?" Hope stood next to him, watching his face.

She had come up on his left side, and for the first time in a long time, it didn't bother him. It was probably because he was too tired to care about anything other than food, a shower, and sleep. He shouldn't be so happy to see her. But he could feel the corners of his mouth turning up on their own accord.

"Just happy to be home." Once the guys had crowded around the kitchen table, Tony walked into the kitchen and found an empty seat. A hot bowl of soup was placed in front of him along with a plate stacked with two grilled cheese sandwiches. It was like when he was a kid and his mom made him lunch on cold days. The day had been anything but cold; however, the meal was perfect.

The second Jerod had finished saying grace, all of the men dug in and ate heartily. In fact, Dana and Hope had to pull out several bags of chips in order to satisfy their hunger. They really had worked up an appetite. Missing lunch hadn't helped. And now that it was basically dinner, most of them probably wanted something a bit more substantial. However, he couldn't blame Dana for not having steak ready for them. Since they weren't able to contact her, she wouldn't have known when, or if, they were coming back that night.

"Ladies, thank you for a wonderful meal." Jerod nodded and started to get up from the table.

"Uh, uh, uh. Not so fast, mister. You still haven't told us what happened today." Dana pursed her lips and glared at her husband. "I waited patiently while everyone ate. Now, spill it."

Jerod winced as he sat back down. "Sorry. As you know, there's a fire not too far away in Idaho. It's slowly making its way here. Firefighters have been called in from all over the country to help battle the blaze. It's a really bad one."

"Will it reach us?" Fear tinged Dana's voice, but she wasn't going to let this bring her down.

Jerod shook his head. "I really don't know. There's already over one hundred thousand acres burned. It's moving fast. We need rain and zero wind to stop it."

"Sounds like we need a miracle," Hope added.

"That would be about it." Tony nodded his agreement.

"We did hear about it. So how did that keep you out so long, and where did you go? I tried calling you a few times over the radio but couldn't get you."

Tony wasn't surprised Dana had tried calling them, and he also wasn't surprised they'd never heard her. They had gone pretty far away.

A sour expression crossed Jerod's face as he began their story. "We had been checking the fence lines to make sure that there wasn't anything along them to create a fire hazard."

"See, I told you." Hope stared at her cousin and crossed her arms over her chest.

Dana rolled her eyes heavenward.

Jerod chuckled. "So, we got to the back of the property and found a gaping hole in the fence and a dozen or so cattle grazing on our ground as though nothing was wrong. I sent Mike back to get supplies to fix the fence and the rest of us started herding the cattle back onto the neighbor's side."

Skeeter picked up the story. "Once the fence was fixed, we cleaned up our mess and was about to head home when we heard something."

"A scream for help," Tony added.

All the men exchanged worried looks at the table, and Jerod picked up where Tony had left off. "We opened the fence line, again, and headed through. Mike did a make-shift fix behind us."

"To make sure the cattle didn't go back through." It'd been the first time since they'd arrived home that Mike Blankenship had spoken. "I didn't want the cows to hurt themselves, or get lost." He shrugged.

"Anyway, we went in search of the noise and discovered our neighbor, Mr. Langston, on the ground with a broken ankle."

Hope and Dana both inhaled loudly.

"Oh, no. Is he alright?" Dana put a hand over her heart.

Tony had only met the man once before that day, but he thought Mr. Langston was a tough nut and he'd be alright.

"I'm sure he will be. We had to stabilize the ankle and leg. Then we built a sort of pull cart from what we could find and brought him back to his house. His wife was all in a tizzy so we waited with her until the ambulance came." Jerod gave a sheepish look to his wife.

"Why didn't you call me once you were within range?" Now, Dana sounded indignant.

But, to be fair, she had a point.

To help his friend, Tony spoke up, "We weren't really thinking too much about anything else. You see, there was also a brush fire on the Langston land. Jerod and I waited at the house while the rest of the men went back out to stop the fire from spreading."

"Oh, no. Please tell me that the Idaho fire hasn't made it that far?" Tears began to form in Hope's eyes.

Tony wondered if she'd been through a fire before. It wasn't like being at a bonfire. The heat from a wildfire could incapacitate a victim before the flames ever arrived. And when the smoke was factored in, let's just say most people died from smoke inhalation and not from the fire itself, thankfully.

"No, it's not here. Today was just one more reason why we need rain. A brush fire can start anywhere when it's dry enough. Which is why beginning tomorrow, we'll be checking our land and offering to help all of our neighbors check theirs for large sections of brush. We all have to be better prepared to prevent a wildfire on our land." Jerod was about to say more, but Skeeter cut him off.

"Does that mean no more burning trash?" The young man looked at Jerod with a serious expression Tony had never seen on him before.

"Exactly. Thank you for bringing that up, Skeeter." The man of the house turned to his wife. "Dana, until further notice, we'll have to bag up our trash and store it in the bins. When they get full, one of us will take it to the dump.

No burning anything, not even a barbecue or a tiny pit fire. Not until the danger passes."

"I did notice the no-burn signs when I was on my way over today." Hope looked around at the table. "I think the fire department is already working to ensure that we don't have any unnecessary dangers."

"That's good to hear. Now, why don't we all go get cleaned up and relax for the evening? Tomorrow is going to be another hot day, and very busy with fire prevention." This time when Jerod stood, no one stopped him.

Tony took his time getting up. He knew that all the men wanted to shower, but the ranch didn't have a water heater big enough for them all to shower at the same time. Nor did they have enough showers. Only three at a time could use the facilities. He could wait. Besides, he wanted to take the opportunity to speak with Hope.

When Hope turned away from him and began cleaning the kitchen table, Tony wondered if she wasn't ready to talk to him. But that wasn't fair. She was cleaning up. Instead of letting himself worry, he decided to help the ladies. It was rare that any of the men offered to help without first being prodded.

"Can I help?" Tony picked up his plate and bowl, then added the setting next to his. When they had the table cleared, he also helped them in the kitchen.

The ranch had a decent dishwasher. And Tony knew that Dana utilized it as much as possible, but not all the dishes fit. While Dana rinsed the dishes that did go into the machine, he and Hope stood off to the side discussing who would wash the pots and pans and who would dry.

"Why don't I wash since I don't know where everything goes." Hope looked at the small pile of larger pots and pans that would need to be washed by hand.

"I suppose I could do that." Tony hoped they would get some time alone, but he wasn't sure if Dana would leave them to finish the dishes without her.

It really was too bad they didn't have a second sink in the kitchen, then Dana could rinse the smaller dishes while Tony and Hope washed the rest.

It seemed destiny was on their side, or Skeeter was.

"Dana? Where's the rest of the clean towels?" Skeeter yelled out from down the hall.

With a heavy sigh and glance to the sky, Dana's lips moved, but no sound came out. Then she looked at Hope and Tony. "Be right back."

"Don't hurry on our part. We've got this." Tony said a quiet thanks to God for arranging an opportunity for them to be alone.

Neither of them spoke as Hope began filling one side of the sink with warm, soapy water. Tony took a towel out of the drawer and stood off to the side waiting for the first pot to be cleaned.

"So, how do you feel? You know, after today?" Hope's voice was hesitant, and she kept her eyes on the task at hand.

Tony wasn't sure, but he thought she sounded nervous. Truth be told, he was as well. "Fine, now that my belly is full." A nervous chuckle erupted from his lips. "I guess once I get my shower I'll feel even better."

"You don't have to help me. You can go get cleaned up if you want." Again, Hope kept her eyes averted as she spoke to him.

He couldn't be sure, but it sounded as though she didn't want him there. "Well, I can't yet. I'll be last tonight and by the time it gets around to my turn, the hot water will be gone, so I most likely won't shower for at least another hour or two."

The idea that she may not want him around sent a pang through his heart. While Tony knew he wasn't ready for a relationship, there was still a pull toward this beautiful woman that he couldn't ignore.

Even if he wanted to.

Chapter 17

T ony had been right. About the hot water. By the time Hope was down to her last pan to rinse, the water was barely lukewarm. She doubted the shower would even be that warm if anyone jumped in before the water heater had time to do its job.

She thought it would be weird being alone with Tony. And when Dana had left them, she'd almost run after her cousin. But after the first few minutes, it felt natural. They got into a rhythm, and the conversation flowed easily. It probably helped that they weren't speaking about anything serious, or heavy.

"Did you get a chance to take a ride today?" Tony dried the last pot while Hope emptied the dirty water in the sink. She'd wait until later to turn on the dishwasher. It used hot water for part of the cycle, and she'd rather save any that might be squeezed out of the old water heater for the guys, especially Tony.

It took a moment for Hope to realize he'd asked her a question. Her mind had been stuck on the hot water issue. "Ride?" She looked up. "Oh, no. I arrived and Dana was already starting to worry about you guys." She grinned. "Especially Jerod."

He chuckled. "Sounds about right. But I'm sorry you missed out on a ride. Dana said your horse was lame? Will she be alright?"

"I hope so. Juniper's been limping the past couple of days. When the vet looked at her, he taped her left rear fetlock. He said to let her rest for the week. Then see how she moves around the corral." Hope couldn't think of what might have caused the issue, maybe she had ridden her mare too hard? She would have to pay closer attention to the animal.

"Does she love to have her head when you're out galloping?" The question brought her up short. Tony must have known her mare.

"Yes, that's exactly it. When we're out, she loves it when I let her loose to run as fast as she wants. I enjoy it, too." A memory of their last ride made Hope think that must have been it. When they were close to the barn, Juniper had slowed much earlier than normal and seemed almost hesitant to keep going. She should have iced the mare's legs at that point. But Juniper wasn't showing any signs of distress other than wanting to go slow.

"I'm sure with rest and the bandage Juniper will be good as new. I just wish you could have gone out riding here today." Tony put the last pan in the cupboard and then set out the towel to dry.

"Yeah, me too. But I'm really glad I was here for my cousin. I don't know how she would have gotten through the afternoon if she'd been all alone." It wasn't until that moment that Hope realized it was providence, or possibly

God's hand, that had brought her there when she'd arrived. If Juniper hadn't been on rest, then Hope wouldn't have even thought to go over to ride with Dana that day.

"Why don't you come back tomorrow evening and we can go for a ride?"

Tony's question brought Hope up short. Was he asking her out on a date? Or just a friendly ride? She felt her hands shake as she thought about it. Just as she was about to turn him down, he spoke up.

"It's not a date, mind you. I was just thinking that we could go for a ride like friends do." Tony looked away, but before he did, Hope thought she caught sight of pink on his cheeks.

If he was embarrassed, what did that mean? A zing of exhilaration shot through Hope, but she reminded herself that she wasn't in the market for a boyfriend, or even a date. "Riding as friends sounds really nice. How about four o'clock?"

A sound from behind them caught Hope's attention, and she turned around to see Dana trying to stifle a laugh. So, her cousin had been eavesdropping. She'd have to find a way to get back at her.

"So, what did I miss?" A huge grin spread across Dana's face, and Hope shook her head.

If Dana started teasing her in front of Tony, well, Hope would find some way to get her back, and good.

"We finished the washing. But I wouldn't start the dishwasher until right before you go to bed." Maybe Hope could find a way to do something to the dishes? Put a red pack of paint in there? No, that might ruin the dishwasher. While Hope did have a strong need to get her cousin back, she didn't want to destroy anything. She had seen a few ideas on Pinterest recently.

"Uh, huh. What else?" Dana winked at Hope.

A feeling of unease spread across Hope's back. She prayed Tony hadn't seen the wink.

"I think Hope's gonna come back tomorrow night to try and get her ride in." While Tony didn't mention the ride would be with him, he did move a couple of steps closer to Hope, making it look like he was laying claim.

While the idea of him liking her was sweet, she really hoped he was just lending her moral support.

And nothing more.

Chapter 18

The smoke hung around the valley all night and all the next day. In fact, the weather service had issued a health warning. The haze was so thick and putrid, she couldn't even see the mountains in the distance. Hope worried she wouldn't be able to go on a ride that evening if things kept up like this. It might be too difficult for the horses to breathe.

But she was too excited to stay home. Instead, she confirmed with Dana via text message that she was still welcome to come over. In addition to the invitation, Dana teased her over Tony again. Now Hope was really going to have to get her cousin back. Things were starting to feel just like old times.

When they were young, they'd played small practical jokes on each other. The worst thing they had done was Hope putting Dana's bra in the freezer overnight. Hope felt bad when tears pooled in Dana's eyes the next morning. It was her only clean bra.

Hope had thought they'd put aside their little pranks long ago. So when Dana texted Hope's *boyfriend* was planning a picnic, it only meant one thing: it was game on. Hope eagerly looked up the pranks she'd tagged on Pinterest and grabbed a few supplies to put in her backpack before leaving.

But as she drew near the ranch, all thoughts of pranks fled. The only thing she could think about was going riding.

Riding with Tony.

Her heart fluttered as an image of the two of them riding off into the sunset flooded her mind. The sun was low in the sky, but it still provided plenty of light for them to see the beauty of God's creation. The further down the sun went, the darker the oranges became until it was almost a purple sky with streaks of orange and red barely visible over the mountaintops in the west.

Gone was the smoke from the fires. The air was crisp and clean, and a light breeze fluttered through the trees. The crickets serenaded them as Tony stopped next to a small creek. Hope brought her horse up so close he was able to reach out and take hold of her hand. They sat there on their mounts, watching as the last of the orange and red melted away from the painted sky only to be replaced by navy-blues, purples, and twinkling stars. Nothing was as beautiful as a Montana sky.

Abruptly, Hope was jerked out of her daydream. Reality was nothing like what she had just dreamt. The sky was still filled with smoke that blocked out most of the sun's rays. Instead of a beautiful pallet of colors, all she could see was gray. And the smell? Whew! It was so strong, her nose twitched.

One thing was for sure, she wasn't going to let any horse gallop in this air. They'd have to take a sedate walk, only going far enough to give the horses some exercise, then bring them back. If only the winds would change and the smoke blown out to sea.

By the time she reached the end of the Crooked Arrow's drive, both Tony and Dana were on the front porch waiting for her.

Tony walked down the steps, his expression blank. Hope had no idea what he was thinking, or what he would say when he greeted her.

"Good evening. How are you today?" Tony helped her down out of her tank of a truck.

"I'm fine, thank you. And you?" With the pleasantries out of the way, Hope prayed he'd say something to let her know what he was thinking.

"Just a bit worried about the air quality. We won't be able to go far, or let the horses have their heads. Are you fine with that?" Tony put her hand in the crook of his arm, like one of those old-fashioned gentleman ranchers she'd heard so much about.

The feel of his arm made her giddy, and she hoped it meant they really would get to have their picnic, after all. She had skipped dinner for this.

Tony looked up to the west and grimaced. Hope followed his gaze, but all she could see was smoke. The mountains would be covered in various shades of greens and browns this time of year, but the horizon was nothing but haze. Hope was no painter, but she sure did enjoy the beauty of the land. Too bad today held no beauty to gaze upon.

Well, maybe one beauty. Tony looked as though he had just jumped out of the shower. His blond hair went below his collar and curled a bit at the ends. Hope guessed he kept his hair a bit longer to cover up the scars, and the missing part of his ear. But that didn't bother her. Her only concern was how he felt about it.

The man was just as gorgeous as any cover model. His blonde hair and turquoise blue eyes could catch any woman's attention. And his smile, boy howdy! When he smiled, really and truly smiled, it lit up his face and warmed everyone around him. Sadly, Tony didn't smile very much. At least not a real smile. He tried; she'd seen his lips curl up many times. But the emotion that normally accompanied a smile rarely made it to his eyes.

Hope mentally shook herself out of the fog her mind was in and focused on the moment. "I think it will be fine if we take a short ride, and don't let the horses work too hard. They do need some exercise, even when the air is so rotten."

"We could have our picnic out back before we leave, if you like?" Tony didn't look excited by the offer. His eyes were a bit glazed over, and his lips were in a flat line.

"How about we ride out to the creek and let the horses graze while we sit down for the picnic? Then come back. That way we can at least enjoy some of the beauty this land has to offer." It would also give Hope more time with Tony, alone. She knew Dana wasn't going to join them. But if they had their picnic in the back yard, most of the residents would find a way to join them.

Even though Hope knew this wasn't a date, it was just two friends hanging out, she still wanted the time alone with Tony. They'd lost out on an entire month. If they were away from prying eyes and ears, maybe he'd open up to her about what he'd been going through.

"I like that idea." The smile Tony gave made it feel as though the skies were clear and the sun was shining down upon them both.

She felt her smile through her entire body. Before Hope could let her imagination roam again, Dana walked up and broke the mood. Hope was partly glad for the interruption, and a small part of her wanted to shoo her cousin away. All these conflicting emotions were starting to grate on Hope's nerves. She needed to keep them in check and remember—only friendship.

"So, you two decide where you're gonna go?" Her cousin lifted one side of her mouth in a sly grin as she swayed from side to side.

Hope was certain Dana would wink at her any moment. So she narrowed her eyes in a warning to her cousin to knock it off.

"As a matter of fact, yes." Tony didn't say more, he just took Hope by the hand and led her around the house, back to the barn.

Dana started to follow, but stopped when Jerod called for her.

Once the two of them were safely inside the barn, Hope let loose the breath she'd been holding. "Do you think anyone else will try to join us?"

Tony frowned, which only made Hope think he wanted to be alone as well. "I hope not. But these guys..." He trailed off, shaking his head.

"Yeah, I hear ya." Dana was just as nosy. Then a thought crossed Hope's mind, one she had to share. "How are you with practical jokes?"

Tony laughed. "I love them."

Hope told him her various ideas as they readied the horses. She also noted a full picnic basket sitting on the table in the tack room, just waiting for them. A picnic was still a picnic no matter if it was shared in the back yard or by a creek, and Hope was thrilled he'd planned it.

And she was doubly thrilled he'd jumped at her offer to relocate to the creek. It would be the first time they'd really get to be alone together. Make that triply thrilled.

Chapter 19

The darkening sky had Tony worried, but not for the fire. He knew it was still a ways away; he was concerned for the lack of light. While he had attached a lantern to his saddlebag, they'd have to be careful riding back to the barn. They'd have enough light to eat, but not much for getting home.

Home. The Crooked Arrow and Frenchtown really did feel like home to him. Especially since he was now persona non grata with his own family. Okay, okay, so maybe it wasn't exactly that he wasn't welcome. No, it was they were uncomfortable having him around with his injuries. Over the past month he'd dealt with his new normal.

New normal, pft. Who ever came up with that phrase, and made it acceptable, had never dealt with so much change before. He hated his future prospects. But he did have a skillset that he could use and stay out of the public eye. Maybe his dad could use him back on their family ranch?

He shook his head. Now wasn't the time to think about his future. Now was the time to think about…well, now. He needed to be in the moment since he was out riding with Hope. Although, he couldn't help chuckle when he thought about the future pranks Hope wanted him to help her with.

"What's so funny?" Hope's borrowed horse was only a few paces away from Tony, close enough to hear him chuckle.

Tony turned his head to look at her. "I was just thinking about the various ways to get Dana back and how the men of the ranch are also going to enjoy it."

"Oh, really? You think they'll get in on the action?" Hope wasn't sure she wanted to get all of them involved in her retribution. It might be too much. And besides, the more who knew about it, the bigger the chances were of Jerod finding out and stopping it.

"No." Tony shook his head and grinned. "I think a few of those pranks of yours will work on the guys as well."

"Ah, I see. So, the men of the Crooked Arrow need a bit of payback, too, huh?" The idea intrigued Hope. Not only would she be able to prank Dana, but she'd end up spending more time with Tony.

"You got it. What do you say? Should we spread the net even further than you originally planned?"

Hope grinned and nodded. "This is going to be so much fun."

It didn't take long to get to the little creek. Once they found a good place to set their blanket, they stopped and dismounted. Tony took their reins and tied the horses to a tree that was close enough to the water so they could drink, and there was just enough grass left that they could snack.

In Hope's pack was an apple for each horse, a little treat for them while she and Tony enjoyed their picnic. As Tony set out the blanket and the contents of his basket, she reached into her pack and gave the horses their treat.

"That was really nice of you to think of them." Tony stood and watched her run her hands down the neck of each horse after she gave them an apple.

Once she was done scratching behind the ears of her borrowed horse, she turned to see Tony watching her with a dazed expression on his face. She felt heat run up her neck and pool in her cheeks. The way he looked at her made her think he might be just as attracted to her as she was to him.

But that was foolish thinking, and she turned away before he could see the heat in her eyes. She needed to cool down and remind herself that nothing could happen. He wasn't ready, and neither was she. They were just friends. Hope repeated that mantra in her head a few times before she felt she had her heart under control.

Then, when she was ready, she joined him on the blanket. "Wow, this is a nice spread. Did you make it?"

In front of them was a platter of fresh fruit, two water bottles, two chicken salad sandwiches, and four chocolate chip cookies.

"I gathered it. Does that count?" The whites of Tony's teeth sparkled when he grinned at her.

"I take it Dana helped?"

Tony reached for a bottle of water and handed it to Hope. "She made the sandwiches and cookies. But I put the fruit plate together and packaged it all up. I'm not completely clueless when it comes to packing a picnic."

"I never said you were." Hope took a drink of the water and sighed. "It's still so nice and cold. Thank you."

In between bites, they planned exactly when and where they'd play their pranks.

When they moved onto the cookies, Hope pulled her backpack into her lap. "I've actually got one small prank with me." She pulled out the items and grinned.

The look on Tony's face told Hope he wasn't following.

"Take the large Styrofoam cup and write on it." She turned it upside down and wrote, *GIANT spider inside. Need a strong man to kill it.* Then she poked a hole in the cup and held the bits of Styrofoam in her hand. "I'll put this on the ground near the kitchen so Dana will see it. Then spread out the bits of Styrofoam so it looks like the spider got out."

Tony chuckled. "I take it Dana hates spiders."

Hope held her stomach as she laughed. "She's sooo totally afraid of them. When we were kids, she'd scream and run in the opposite direction if she even saw a spider web."

"Huh, does that mean she hates Spiderman?" One of Tony's favorite comic book heroes was Spiderman. He thought the recent movies were the best ones so far, even though they were pretty different from the classic comics.

Hope chuckled. "Not at all. She loves Spiderman, and all of the superheroes. But my favorite is Thor." A dreamy look passed over her face as she sighed. She'd always been a fan of Thor, but the moment she saw Chris Hemsworth wielding his hammer, she was in love.

Tony smiled. For the first time in a very long time, he was having a normal conversation with a woman. And if they were on a date, it would have been a normal date. If things continued, he was on his way to being a totally normal guy once more.

Hope really enjoyed the light-hearted banter with Tony. She couldn't remember one single date with any man that had been this fun, and innocent. Although, it wasn't truly a date, so maybe that was why it was so much fun? She was being herself, not worried about impressing a guy. And there was no pressure to do anything more than what she was comfortable with. Men in this day and age always wanted one thing. And when she didn't give it to them, they usually called her names and moved on.

That was until… Well, she wasn't going to think about him.

Instead, she decided to just enjoy being friends with Tony. No more of this back and forth does she like him, no, she can't. They were friends. Period. End of story.

"Well, I suppose we should start heading back. It's dark, and is it is me, or is the smoke getting thicker?" Tony stood up and held a hand out to help Hope to her feet.

Hope took in a deep breath and coughed. "I think I'm about to cough up a lung, it's so bad now. Let's get back." They weren't very far from the main house, since the ranch didn't own much land. But it did take them almost twenty minutes to get back to the barn. They had to stop a few times and look good and hard to get their bearings.

Thankfully, Tony knew this ranch like the back of his hand. A tree here, a rock there, and he knew which direction the barn was.

And it was a good thing they made it home when they did. Jerod had a scowl on his face when he greeted them at the barn. "Do you know how dangerous it is to be out in the smoke at night?"

"Whoa, we weren't far. The horses didn't even canter, it was a slow walk for us all." Tony dismounted and glared at the ranch owner.

"I'm not worried about the horses. I was worried about you two. The fire has gotten too close for comfort." The frown on Jerod's face was deep, wrinkles forming around his mouth and eyes. Wrinkles Hope hadn't seen before.

"We're not in any danger, are we?" Hope tried to take in a deep breath, but the smoke clogged up her lungs and she coughed.

"This"—Jerod pointed at Hope—"is exactly why I didn't want you out in this."

"Jerod, I hate to break it to you, but it doesn't matter where I am, I'm gonna cough when the air is so bad." Hope rubbed at the pain beginning in her chest.

"Well, come on, then. Dana has some tea that should help you both clear your lungs out. And we'll put on the air purifiers we have in the house." Jerod led them all back to the house.

By the time Hope left, she was feeling much better. Not just because her cough had lessened, but because she was beginning to see a true friendship develop between her and Tony. And he wasn't nearly as self-conscious anymore around her. In fact, he had turned his left side to her for little bit.

All in all, it was a good day.

Chapter 20

For the next few days, the fire inched closer and closer to Frenchtown. Then, as if God himself decided to change the course of the fire, it turned north and even began to die down a little.

Tony had been going stir-crazy. The only work they were allowed to do was tend the animals. However, each day Jerod did take one of the guys with him, along with a radio, and they slowly rode the fence lines, ensuring no sparks were anywhere near their land.

The only bright part was Hope had come over for dinner the past two nights. And today was Sunday. They'd all be in church together.

Having a female friend who wasn't a girlfriend, or on her way to being a girlfriend, was new for Tony. Sure, in high school there were girls in his group, but most of them either wanted to date him, or he wanted to date them. This was the first time as an adult that Tony had a true friend who was a woman. And a beautiful one at that.

He was growing and healing. Which was really nice. Even Megan had said he was doing much better. Shoot,

Tony hadn't even had a nightmare in over two weeks. Things were looking up, and he was feeling pretty good. In fact, the next day he had a phone call with his doctor to determine when he could have his final surgery.

When they all arrived at church, Tony didn't even think twice about sitting in the back, or staying in the entryway, like he had once done. Now, he had a regular seat up close, but still on the side. He liked being close enough to read the pastor's lips, should he need a little extra help in discerning what was being said.

Before the service began, Tony went down to the front to take his favorite seat and was surprised to see Nelly and Sam sitting there. She had Rogue, as usual, between them. But Buffy was also in attendance.

"Hi, Nelly." Tony nodded to Sam. "Are you training Buffy for church?" He wasn't sure why Buffy was there that day. Nelly didn't usually bring the other dogs to church.

"Hi, Tony. I thought I'd bring Buffy to see you. I think she misses you." Nelly scooched over so there was room for Tony to sit by her and Buffy.

Even Sam seemed to want them there. "Take a seat, man. Church is about to start." He pointed to the pulpit where the assistant pastor stood to begin the service.

Not wanting to be rude, Tony took a seat and put his hand on Buffy's head. He did like the dog; she was sweet and helpful. And if he was honest, he'd missed her the past few days. Even Nelly had wanted to stay close to home, just in case the fire got too close and she needed to evacuate.

After the opening prayer, the assistant pastor asked everyone to keep praying for the safety of their firefighters, and for God to send rain. It was going to take a miracle to stop the fire. "Also, I think it's appropriate to thank God for moving the fire away from Frenchtown. Let's continue to pray that the fire misses homes and businesses until it's put out."

Tony could get behind that thought one hundred percent. Once the singing was over and the pastor was in the pulpit preaching, Tony relaxed his shoulders and listened intently to the message.

Partway through the sermon, Buffy had put her head on his knee, and he'd put his hand on her head. Tony didn't even realize what they'd done until it was time to stand and sing the invitation song. "Hey, girl." He scratched behind her ears. "Did you like the sermon?"

The dog looked lovingly up at Tony, and her tongue lolled to the side. She stayed quiet, not even a low chuff, as the service concluded. When he stood to leave, Buffy trailed him down the aisle and out the door.

Nelly and Sam stood back, watching the duo. "He doesn't even realize it, does he?" She asked her boyfriend.

Sam shook his head. "No, but he needs to."

Hope watched Tony and Buffy walk toward her. She smiled at Tony and looked down at Buffy who was a couple of steps behind Tony. He must not have realized she was there, because when he noticed where Hope was looking, he frowned and turned around.

"Buffy?" Not really knowing what to think, he leaned down and patted her head. "I think you're supposed to be with Nelly, not me." He smiled at the dog.

But Buffy wasn't having any of it. She chuffed and walked to his left side and stood there. She was a woman on a mission. A mission to stay with Tony.

"I think someone has a new friend." Hope looked from dog to man and back to dog again. "Dontcha, girl?" She leaned over and rubbed Buffy's head. The dog didn't have her service vest on, so Hope was free to pet her.

"I love dogs. And I think female dogs are the best companions. Unlike their male counterparts." Hope eyed Rogue. "They don't have the need to pee everywhere and claim their territory."

Nelly, Sam, and Tony all chuckled.

"I do think it's nice to have a female dog," Tony admitted.

Buffy must have understood, for she nudged Tony's leg and chuffed her agreement.

Tony looked around. "Is there something going on that I should know about?" He had spent a lot of time with Buffy. And she did seem to help him over the past month, quite a bit, in fact. But he didn't think he needed a full-time companion, no matter how great Buffy was. There were other wounded vets out there who needed a dog much more than he did.

Nelly put a hand on Tony's arm. "I know you don't think you need a service dog, but Buffy has chosen you."

"What if I don't want her?" Tony practically whispered his response to ensure he didn't hurt Buffy's feelings. He knew she was smart, like wicked smart. Even though dogs couldn't talk in a human tongue, they understood what humans said.

"You have the right to turn down her offer of service." Nelly bit her lower lip and sighed. "But if I were you, I'd think long and hard before you do. Once you say no, there's no changing your mind."

"I'm going to have another surgery, what happens to Buffy while I'm in the hospital?" This was one more reason Tony didn't think he needed a dog. Once he had his surgery, he'd be doing so much better. And he didn't have a place to keep her while he was in the hospital.

"As I understand it, you'll be coming back here to the ranch once you're released from the hospital, right?" Nelly asked.

Tony nodded.

Nelly smiled and spread her hands. "Then it's simple, I'll watch her until you return."

Tony chewed on her words as they all made their way outside. Did he really want a dog? It was a lot of responsibility. But Buffy was more than just a responsibility; she was a true partner. Maybe, just maybe, if he accepted what she was offering, he wouldn't feel such a strong pull to Hope. He hadn't said it out loud, but he knew he was lonely and needed companionship. That was probably why he felt so drawn to Hope. But what if Buffy provided him with a true partner? Not a romantic one, but a day-to-day partner that would help lighten his load?

Could this be the answer he needed? Would Buffy make it possible for him to continue being friends with Hope without the constant want to hold her in his arms and kiss her all night long?

Buffy seemed to understand his hesitancy, and she nudged his left thigh. But when Tony looked down, he caught something else out of the corner of his eye. A ball was coming right at him.

His Army training provided him with the reflexes to turn and catch it before it could hit him. "Oof." Whoever had thrown it at him had given it some real heat. He looked around for the culprit.

Then he noticed a teenager looking everywhere but him. The tension in his shoulders loosened, and he made his way over—with Buffy on his left.

"Hey, there. This yours?" Tony held the football out to the young man.

"Uh, yes, sir. I'm sorry." The boy still refused to look him in the eye.

"What happened?" From the way the boy acted, he doubted the kid had tried to hurt him.

Buffy took two steps closer and sniffed the boy's legs. Then she walked back to Tony. When she sat and waited for Tony to do something, he knew she'd checked the boy out and hadn't found anything wrong with him. Dogs could sense if someone had malicious intent, and they didn't even need to be trained. It was just something innate in all dogs.

A slow grin spread across his face. "Is your aim that poor?"

That got the boy's dander up. "No, sir. I'm the quarterback on our high school team."

"Then what happened?"

The boy sighed and rolled his head around. "I was playing catch and Jason, my buddy, missed."

Trying to hold back a laugh, Tony nodded. "I see. I take it you have a lot of power in that arm of yours. Maybe next time you can wait until you're not around a bunch of people before throwing the ball? That could have hurt someone."

The boy winced when he looked up at Tony. Whether from guilt, or from finally noticing the scars on Tony's face, he wasn't certain. But he knew the boy got the message.

"I'm sorry, sir. I won't do it again."

"Good, see that you don't. And I'll look forward to seeing you play this fall." While Tony wasn't a big high school football fan, he was curious about this boy's talent.

After he returned the ball to the boy, Tony turned to walk away. Without a single word or hand gesture, Buffy followed him. When they were back with Nelly and Sam, Tony leaned down. *"Braver hund."*

"Looks like Buffy can do a lot to help you." Sam had stayed quiet for most of the conversation, but now it seemed he had an opinion. "I think having Buffy will be very good for you. She's really taken to you, and like she just proved, she's looking out for you. Even when she's not on duty."

"You know, I think you might be right." Uncertainty still nagged at him though. "If you had it to do all over again, would you still take Rogue?"

Sam put his hand down on his dog's head. "In a heartbeat. In fact, I'd do it sooner. If only I knew then what I know now." He leaned down and hugged his dog. No, scratch that, his partner.

Tony had seen enough of the interaction between Sam and Rogue to know they were true partners. While Rogue may have been a dog, he was so much more than a pet.

And the changes that had come about in Sam since accepting Rogue were undeniable. Sam was a completely new man. Of course, having Nelly as his girlfriend didn't hurt.

But Tony had seen the look of pure pleasure, and love, Sam had given Rogue, and vice versa. The two had a bond so much stronger than owner and pet. And when Tony noticed Sam getting upset, he also noticed how Rogue would come closer. Sam would put his hand down on the dog, and the lines of worry on his face would fade and erase.

There was something between a service dog and a human that Tony didn't understand and couldn't put into words. In fact, he didn't think Nelly could put it into words, either.

"What if I say yes, and then change my mind?" Tony wasn't the sort to make a decision lightly. And if he committed, then he committed. That was part of the problem with his uncle.

The man had promised him a position, not to mention the entire company. It really hurt that his uncle was going back on his word. Tony wouldn't go back on his word to Buffy, but he needed to know all the repercussions of any decision.

Nelly scratched her chin. "It's not that easy. Once a dog bonds with a human, and the human accepts the gift…it would be like a divorce. I know the relationship between partners isn't romantic, and it's nothing like what humans do with each other. It's so much more intense. I doubt Buffy would bond with anyone else if you accepted her only to turn your back on her down the road."

He hadn't thought of how it might affect the dog. "Okay, say I accept Buffy and we totally gel. What happens if I die before her?"

Nelly's shoulders drooped, and her eyes clouded over. "Is there something you aren't telling me?"

Confusion furrowed Tony's brow. "Huh?" Then it hit him. "Oh, no. I don't have anything that's going to end my life soon. At least, I don't think I do. But what if I'm in an accident or something?"

"Generally, in those situations, a family member or friend will take the dog and she'll become more of a pet then a partner. A service dog will rarely bond again. Especially if they've been with their human a long time. This is a lifetime commitment."

Nelly's words pierced Tony's aching heart. This was what he wanted, someone to love him unconditionally. But didn't the Lord already do that? Then why was he looking for that sort of love here on Earth? Maybe he was really broken and needed a service dog.

Tony put his hand on Buffy's head. "Alright, what do I gotta do?"

Chapter 21

"Shh, they'll hear you." Trying her best to stifle a giggle, Hope put a finger to her lips and crept past the front window with Tony and Buffy on her heels.

Tony was doing his best to keep from laughing.

Only Buffy was being very quiet. It was as though she understood what they were doing, and approved. The smart dog stuck right to Tony's left side and nudged him when he was too close to a small rock, even though Tony had seen it.

"I can't believe we're actually doing this." Though he was speaking in hushed tones, Tony still put a hand over his mouth.

Stealing a peek through the window, they discovered the majority of the ranch residents watching TV in the living room. The game was on, and the TV blared loud enough to wake the dead. It muffled their sneaking perfectly.

The moment they were around the corner of the house, Hope stood up. "Whew, that was close. We should have gone the long way around."

"But then Dana would have surely seen us. She's in the kitchen cleaning up. You know she would have." Tony stood next to Hope, holding a bag of supplies.

Their first prank, the one with the Styrofoam cup and fake spider, had been a dud. Dixon had found it and picked it up. He laughed when he threw it away, but didn't seem to know who had done it.

This time, they were going for something a bit more scary. And something that everyone had a chance to see— glowing eyes outside the bedroom windows.

Earlier in the day, Hope and Tony had cut freaky eyes out of toilet paper rolls. Now, they were going to break glow sticks and put them inside the makeshift eyes.

"Whose room is this?" Hope pointed to a window with the blinds open.

"That's mine. We can skip it." Tony started to move forward, but Buffy nudged his thigh to get his attention.

"We have to put them outside all rooms, except for one. Then everyone will think it was that person who did it." A devilish grin crossed Hope's face. She raised her brows once and nodded before placing one of the rolls outside Tony's window.

"You are evil. But I like it. Who are we gonna pin this on?" Tony followed Hope as they made their way to the next window. "This is Dixon's."

Hope stopped and looked at the window. She bit her lip as she considered the targets. "We can't pin it on Dana and Jerod. Skeeter's too obvious." She turned to look at Tony. "Who do you think?"

"You know, I was kinda thinking Mike would be a great one." Tony nodded toward the next one as he placed his roll and light facing the window so the glow would be visible when Dixon went to close his blinds.

"Mike? But he's so quiet." Hope didn't see the nice guy who loved to cuddle with his cows as being a prankster.

"It's always the quiet ones you have to look out for." Tony winked when Hope looked at him.

"Alright, where's his room?"

Tony pointed to the next one. "That's his."

Hope and Tony skipped that window and stopped in front of Skeeter's.

"How about we leave two in front of Skeeter's?" Hope covered her mouth when she started to laugh.

They finished setting up their glowing eyes and walked around the back of the barn to avoid Dana as they made their way to the other side of the house where the master bedroom was located.

Tony walked her to the front where her truck was parked. "Thank you for this. I swear I feel like a teenager again. This was a lot of fun."

Buffy chuffed her agreement.

Hope scratched behind Buffy's ears. "*Braver hund*. You did so well, Buffy. Great job."

The dog licked her hand then sat back on her haunches.

"Well, I guess she agrees?" Hope laughed and this time didn't bother trying to cover the sound. Everyone knew Tony and Buffy walked her out to her truck when she left, so if anyone heard them talking and laughing, they wouldn't think anything was amiss.

"I'd say we both do. Again, thank you for this." He looked around and then whispered. "When do you think we can pull off another prank?"

"Slow down, soldier boy." Hope winked. "Let's see how this one plays out first."

Later that night, Tony was on the phone with Hope, as planned, when everyone began going to bed.

"Do you think you'll hear anything?" Hope asked.

Tony had his door closed, as usual, but the walls were a little thin. "If anyone yells, I'll hear that. But I won't hear Dana or Jerod unless they come running to this side of the house."

"I wonder if it was a mistake to put something outside their win—" Hope quieted when Tony shushed her.

"Listen." He held his phone up as Dixon yelled,

"Who's out there? You better show yourself."

A screeching sound came through the phone and Dana tried to hide her laughter.

Tony whispered into the phone, "Dixon's opening his window."

With a hand over her mouth, Hope giggled. Then she pressed the mute button on her cell phone so she could laugh without anyone hearing.

When cussing came over the line, and the sound of doors slamming, Hope doubled over with laughter, tears pooling in the corners of her eyes.

While she couldn't see what was happening, she sure could imagine. The big, bad soldiers of the Crooked Arrow Ranch were grabbing lamps and baseball bats to confront the evil glowing eyes outside their windows.

Then she heard Tony yell, "What's going on? Who's out there?" His performance was alright, nothing Oscar-worthy. But most likely enough to keep the others from suspecting him.

Tony kept the phone in his hand as he opened his bedroom door. "What's going on?"

In the hallway, Dixon and Skeeter were struggling to put their shirts on as they ran down the hallway.

"Someone's outside my window," Skeeter yelled as he wrestled with his shirt.

Dixon and Sam were right behind him. "Mine, too."

Tony looked around, but didn't see Mike. He grinned and remembered that he had to play along. "Mine, too." He followed the two men and heard more steps behind him. When he turned, he saw an angry scowl on Arthur's face.

Hope was listening in to what was going on around Tony. "This is priceless. I only wish I was there." Her phone rang, signaling that someone was trying to call through on call waiting. She looked down at her phone and froze. It was Dana.

She got herself under control and clicked the button to put Tony on hold while accepting Dana's call. "Dana? What's up?" Hoping she sounded natural, but feeling like she probably sounded guilty, she held her breath and waited.

"Did you see anyone outside the house earlier when you left?" It wasn't fear in Dana's voice; it sounded more like she was angry.

Hope winced and prayed her little prank hadn't cause any serious issues. "No." She paused. "But I think I heard a horse whinny while we were walking to my truck." She hated to lie, but it was all part of the prank, she supposed.

"That's not good," Dana mumbled.

"Why, what's wrong?" Now it was Hope's turn to play her part. If she messed this up for her and Tony, she'd kick herself. A twinge of apprehension stole through her chest, and for one second Hope wondered if they had made a mistake.

"There's these glowing eye things outside my window, and it sounds like the other guys have them too."

"Glowing eyes? You mean like an animal?" She should have looked up what glowing eyes could be before doing this. Now she was just scrambling to cover her tracks.

"No, it can't be. When Jerod opened the window and yelled, the eyes didn't move. They didn't even blink. Jerod thinks it's some dumb prank." Now Dana was starting to sound frustrated.

"Oh, it was probably some of the neighbor kids. You know how it is." Hope giggled and prayed that she'd get Dana to calm down. Dana needed to think it was a neighbor kid and not one of them. The last thing Hope needed was to start a prank war.

Hope and Tony really should have thought this through better. Now that they'd involved everyone else, if anyone figured it out, she and Tony would have the whole house after them.

"Hold on, Jerod wants to go outside and see what it is." Dana took her phone away from her head, but Hope could still hear her. "Be careful, it might be some weird animal."

"Don't worry, I'll take a shotgun." Jerod's bold statement instantly turned Hope's excitement into worry.

"Do you think you'll need a gun?" Hope asked, not knowing if Dana had put the phone back to her ear or not.

Apparently she hadn't.

"Wait for me. I'm coming too." Dana's voice was distant, as though her phone was down by her leg.

Hope wanted to scream, but at the same time she wanted to laugh. She and Tony had got them all from the sound of it. But who would get the blame?

The next thing Hope heard was a group of men all speaking at once. She couldn't understand any of them and wished she could've been the fly on that wall. She also had a sudden hankering for some popcorn.

An idea hit her. "Dana!" she yelled into the phone. When she got no response, she switched back to Tony. "Tony? You there?"

"Yeah, what's up?" His whisper was just barely loud enough for her to hear.

"Call me on FaceTime, I want to see what's going on."

Tony hung up the call and initiated the video call. Hope had to hang up with Dana, but she figured her cousin wouldn't think anything of it.

When the video connection was established, Tony turned the camera around so she could see everyone.

The sight had her laughing all over again. Everyone except for Mike was outside under the night sky, looking around. Jerod had a shotgun slung over his shoulder. Dana was still holding her phone down by her thigh, as though she'd completely forgotten she was supposed to be on a call with Hope.

"Who did this?" Skeeter called out.

"Did what?" Hope yelled.

"Here, I'll show you." Tony winked into the camera before turning it around. Then he walked to the nearest window to show her the toilet paper roll and light coming from within.

A burst of laughter came out from the phone, catching everyone's attention. They all ran to where Tony stood pointing his phone at the ground.

"Is that what's got the whole house in an uproar? Pick it up." Hope laughed again.

Dana scrunched her brows, then looked at her phone and realized that Hope had hung up with her. "Did Hope call you, Tony?"

He turned around, and a sheepish smile crossed his features. "Yes. She wanted to know what was going on, so we're on video chat." He went to pick up the glowing roll outside his own window. The eyes on the roll looked like something one would carve in a pumpkin on Halloween, and a purple light emanated from within.

"It's a glow stick inside of a toilet paper roll." Tony showed it around to everyone.

"Yeah, I got that. But who did it?" Dixon called out.

Tony shrugged.

Jerod looked around. "Where's Mike?"

Skeeter pursed his lips and slapped his thigh. "I bet he did it. That scallywag."

Neither Hope nor Tony were about to say anything to the contrary.

But Sam didn't agree. "I don't know. He's pretty quiet. I can't see him doing this."

"Well, it's late. Grab the lights outside your window and let's all get back to bed." Jerod turned toward his bedroom window with Dana by his side.

Chapter 22

Over the next two days, everyone tried to figure out who was responsible for the glowing eyes. Turns out Mike laughed when confronted with the prank the next day, but everyone believed him when he said he didn't do it. Consensus was that it was a neighbor kid.

To avoid suspicion, Hope and Tony kept to their new routine, which meant an evening ride before suppertime. She sniffed the air. "Smells like the fire might be coming back our way."

"I think it's just the wind. The news said it was almost sixty percent contained. I doubt it would make its way here now." Tony led them along the creek. The water level was almost nonexistent in places, but there were a few little ponds big enough to hold a couple of fish.

"Do you think anyone suspects us?" Hope grinned. While it had been fun playing the joke, a part of her wished they knew it was her and Tony. Or at least suspected.

"Jerod accused everyone one night at the table, and then we all laughed it off. I don't think anyone really cares now.

Even Dana admitted last night that it was a good prank. Probably too good for any of them to have pulled off."

Hope wasn't sure if she should be offended or proud.

"I've got a great picnic packed for tonight. Care to stop here, by the small pond, and have dinner?" Tony had enjoyed their picnic the previous week so much he wanted to do it again. Truth be told, he'd picnic with Hope every night if it wouldn't send the wrong signal.

"Sure, this looks good. Whoa." She pulled on the reins and stopped her horse by a large tree.

Once they were all set up, Tony said grace, and they dished up their plates.

Hope looked up to the sky and pursed her lips. The haze was back and even worse than before. "Did the smoke come in faster this time than last?"

With a pulled pork sandwich halfway to his mouth, Tony paused and looked up. "Nah. I'd say it's about as bad as last week. Are you worried? We could head back if you want."

That was the last thing Hope wanted. She enjoyed being with Tony out on the ranch. It was so peaceful, and he was such a gentleman, nothing at all like her last boyfriend. She scowled every time she thought of Billy. Lately, she'd been doing a lot of personal Bible study on forgiveness and realized that while she had forgiven him, she still hadn't forgiven herself what she had done.

"Why so glum? Is the fire bothering you that much?" Tony put his sandwich back down on his plate and moved to get up, but Hope waved him down.

"No, that's not it at all. I was just thinking about something I shouldn't have been. At least not while we're having such a nice time."

After Tony wiped his face clean with a napkin, he looked at Hope. "We're friends, right?"

Hope nodded.

"And friends confide in each other. So please tell me what's bothering you. Maybe I can help." He leaned over and put a comforting hand on her shoulder.

"It's about my ex. Are you sure you want to hear it?" While Hope didn't mind telling Tony about it, she knew men rarely wanted to hear about a woman's ex-boyfriend, even if they were only friends.

He took a moment to think about it, then he smiled. "If it's bothering you, then I want to help. That's what friends are for."

Hope didn't miss the fact that he mentioned they were only friends twice in quick succession. She wasn't sure why he kept saying it, but it did help her to remember. "Okay, Billy, that's my ex. Well, he was, I mean, is, a very charismatic man. He wooed me right from the start." Hope looked down at the plate in her hands.

"He made me feel wanted, and beautiful. Billy took me out to nice places. And he was always touching me or kissing me. Right away he seemed to think that we were going to get married." Hope stopped and shook her head. "I was such a fool."

"Is marriage important to you?" Tony asked.

She blinked and looked at him. The man didn't look at her as though she was crazy or a nutjob, like so many men had over the years. Instead, he looked her in the eyes, and she could feel the compassion there.

"Yes, it is. But." Hope held up a finger. "It can't be Mr. Right Now, only Mr. Right Forever will do."

"And you thought Billy was the latter?"

"Yeah. And a part of me knew better, but he kept talking about our future and if I loved him I wouldn't make him wait." She threw her hands in the air. "I was so stupid to fall for the oldest trick in the book."

When she looked at Tony, she could tell he was picking up on what she wasn't saying, yet. He pursed his lips and sat there silently waiting for her to continue.

"So, yeah. I slept with him. Even before he gave me a ring. I believed his lies. And I thought he truly loved me and we would get married. In this day and age, a lot of Christian couples do sleep together before marriage, so I didn't think too much of it." Although, she had. That was why she had begun moving further and further from her cousin. Over the past year, Hope had stopped calling Dana, stopped visiting. And she had even sent Dana's calls to voicemail most of the time.

Basically, she ghosted her own cousin. And for what? A lying man.

Still, Tony sat there quietly waiting for her to say more. It started to bug Hope. Did he not have an opinion? Did he have a bad opinion? She wished he would say something, anything. Even if he judged her. She deserved it.

"Aren't you going to say something?" Irritation laced her words, but she didn't care.

"What do you want me to say? That you made a mistake? It's a sin?" He tilted his head. "I think you already know that and have been beating yourself up over it. I don't need to add to your misery."

"You think all that?" She shrank into herself and prayed that Tony wouldn't hate her now. That he'd still want to be her friend.

He shook his head. "I do know pre-marital sex is a sin. But newsflash, I'm not perfect. No human is. It's not my place to judge you." He paused, and a verse came to mind. "Remember when Jesus came upon the adulterous woman and the men of the town were about to stone her?"

"Yeah, John chapter eight." It happened to be part of a recent sermon, one that had been the catalyst for her to make her change.

So when they continued asking him, he lifted up himself and said unto them, He that is without sin among you, let him first cast a stone at her. John 8:7

"Yes, and when they began walking away, Jesus sat there drawing in the dirt. Just waiting to see what the religious leaders would do. And you know what? Not a single one of them remained when Jesus lifted his head." With a grin, Tony picked up his plate and took a bite of his cold, pulled pork sandwich.

"So, you're saying that you won't be casting stones at me." With an ironic tug at her lips, Hope almost smiled.

"Exactly. Who am I to judge you? That's not my job. But it is my job to encourage you to forgive yourself and go to God and pray for His forgiveness. As for me? I'm going to eat my sandwich and continue to be your friend." He took another bite, and once he swallowed, he wiped his mouth. "But I will say that I agree with our decisions to not date for a while. Until you're ready to live by God's standards for dating, you should stay single."

"Thank you." There really wasn't much more to say. Even though Hope knew that Bible story, and had even heard it recently, it wasn't until just now that she realized how much she needed to hear it again.

They spent the next thirty minutes eating and talking about nothing in particular.

When Tony had finished his meal, he cleaned up his plate and put it away. "Hey, do you know what they do around here for fall celebrations? I heard the tree farm has some big plans."

"You know, this is the first year Cody Makinaw and his family will be doing a fall celebration. I heard he's got a pumpkin patch, corn maze, craft fair, and all sorts of fun stuff. I can't wait to see it." Hope's eyes sparkled with excitement, then dimmed when she looked over Tony's shoulder.

Across the creek, she caught sight of something that shouldn't be there. It should be hundreds of miles away. She pointed. "Tony, please tell me that's a mirage, or something shining from the last of the sun?"

He noticed the fear in her eyes, and when he looked back over his shoulder, he, too, felt it snaking up his spine. "Hurry up, leave the picnic. Let's get the horses and hightail it home."

"How did flames get this far?" Hope scrambled to her feet and ran to her horse.

Both horses must have noticed the flames across the creek for they began to paw the ground at their feet. Star, the horse Tony was riding, pulled on her reins and tried to get away.

"Shh, it's alright." Tony put placating hands out to the horse in an effort to calm her down. But it wasn't working. She pulled her reins loose, turned, and ran away as fast as she could.

"Let's get Brownie and we can ride double on her." Hope moved calmly toward her horse and got the reins loose. But the horse was just as antsy and as afraid as Star. She reared up and pulled the reins out of Hopes' hands.

Tony scrambled closer to help her gain control of the mount, but it was too late. Brownie ran in a different direction from Star.

The smoke surrounded them and was so thick, Tony couldn't tell which way to go. "We better grab the drinks and do our best to get back home."

"Can we walk in the creek all the way back?" Hope didn't like the idea of flames anywhere near her. If the fire was just across the small pond, it could mean it was already on their side of the tiny creek.

She knew their only hope was to stick to the water. If they walked through the stream, even when the bed was dry, they would still have a better chance of survival. The bare earth provided no fuel for the fire, and they could douse their bodies in the water. If they could walk the creek all the way back, they just might make it. That didn't mean their lungs would survive, but they could deal with smoke inhalation later.

Tony reached down for the blanket and put it in the water. "Here, let's wrap ourselves with the wet blanket and try to breath through the fibers as much as possible. And we can try, but the creek veers off not far from here and heads toward the Langston ranch."

"As long as it gets us away from the flames, that's all that matters, right?" She pulled the blanket around her and wrapped her left arm around Tony's waist, staying on his right so that he could hear her.

"We'll see." The cryptic tone in Tony's voice sent shivers of fear up and down Hope's spine.

They walked for a few minutes, all the while coughing way too much to be good for either of them.

Hope's throat was already starting to get scratchy, and she worried about the horses' safety. She knew they could find their way home, but would they be able to get home safely in a fire? That thought scared her silly. The only thing she could do now was pray. And she did.

Father, I know you're watching and listening to us. Please, bring us home safely. Don't let anything else happen to Tony, he's been through enough. And help the horses find safe shelter as well. Save the ranch, please, Lord. So many wounded veterans need this place to heal. Don't let it burn, Lord. In Jesus's holy name I pray, amen.

While Hope prayed silently, Tony did the same.

When they had walked about a quarter of a mile downstream, the water began lowering. Tony knew this would happen. The creek bed was always shallow in this section, but in late summer, it would eventually get to a spot where it would be bone dry. "Let's douse ourselves again. The creek dries up just ahead. Then we won't see any more water until we get to the next little pool."

Without saying anything, Hope took the blanket from their shoulders and dropped it into the water, which was barely above their calves. It was a little bit muddy, but that didn't matter at this point. All that mattered was ensuring they stay wet.

Then Tony dropped and rolled in the water, and Hope followed suit. When they stood, Tony picked up the blanket and wrapped it around them.

"Do you want to take a sip of your water bottle now?" Tony took one from his pack and handed it to her.

She shook her head. They might need it later on.

"Come on, at least take a tiny sip. It will help your throat."

She agreed. And Tony took a sip as well.

"How long before we see more water?" Hope asked once they hit the dry part of the creek bed.

The flames were all around them now, and visibility was almost nothing. They both kept the blanket up over their mouths in order to keep as much smoke out of their lungs as possible.

Tony's chest hurt from the deep, wracking coughs, but he was still alive and walking.

Tears ran down Hope's cheeks from the smoke stinging her eyes.

"I don't know. Maybe another fifteen minutes, or more." Tony sent up a quick prayer asking God to put a hedge of protection around them at the same time he squeezed Hope tighter to his right side.

While most of the creek bed was sandy or rocky, there were some dry sprigs coming up from the bed. They caught the attention of the fire roaring not far from their location, and just up ahead, directly in their path, was a small brush fire.

"We have to find a way around it." Tony looked around and saw a small path of dirt. It was just wide enough for them to walk through if they were careful. He wondered if God had cleared that path just for them.

"Tony, I'm afraid." Hope's quiet voice pierced his heart.

He'd had the duty of protecting many souls while in the army, but none were so dear to him as Hope. The idea of failing her now just about stopped his heart. Tony wasn't about to let her die, not here. Not like this.

"Hope, God's protecting us. Look at this path he cleared for us. He's guiding us in the direction he wants us to go, just trust in Him." Easier said than done. Tony did trust God, but it was tough this time. Had it only been him in the fire, he would have been fine not making it back. But Hope? She had too much going for her. An entire life ahead full of love and adventure.

Even if it killed him, he would make sure she made it home safely.

Chapter 23

T ony was right, Hope needed to trust in God to bring them home safely. And while the path wound around, it did seem as though God had put them there. Eventually, they made it back to the creek where a small pool of water waited for them.

"Oh, what a sight for sore eyes. Literally." Hope grinned and dropped the blanket into the pool once the water was up to her thighs. She couldn't believe they had found a pool with so much water still in it. The coolness of the water felt good upon her overheated body. She dunked down underneath and came up only when she ran out of air.

Tony was already standing up, water dripping from his hair, when she opened her eyes. "Do we have to leave this spot?"

"Sadly, yes." He pointed behind her where a wall of fire was making its way to their location. "I don't think the water will last long enough to protect us from that."

Her shoulders drooped when she realized that the fire was circling around them. "We only have that small path."

"Let's go." Tony put the blanket around them, and they slogged through the water until they made it to the edge. Once they were out of the water, they made their way as quickly as they could. His lungs had gone long past aching to where it hurt to breathe now. Even taking shallow breaths hurt. He wondered how Hope was managing.

Lord, if you're going to save us, now would be a wonderful time to do it. While Tony wasn't mad at God, he was a bit miffed at God's timing. He knew God's timing wasn't the same as his, but still. This had gone past dangerous. They were almost fully surrounded by fire. He had no clue how the fire had spread so quickly, and so far, while they were out riding. However, that wasn't what was important.

They had to get to safety, and fast.

"Look, there." Hope pointed to an opening in the fire, where it was only dirt, no brush.

Tony led them that way without a word.

Around them were trees, but somehow there was a clearing that had no brush and no trees. Could this be the fire pit behind the house? He didn't think so. The tree line was too far from the house for this to be it. They had trees near the house, but not a thick cluster like this one.

They weren't far from the creek, so this must be one of the picnic spots the ranch hands had cleared a while back. Jerod had wanted to set up picnic tables and a horseshoe pit, along with a built-in barbecue. He had envisioned lots of Saturday-night barbecues here when the weather was nice. Tony had even helped for some of the work. All they needed were the tables, which were due in any day. Then they could start the dinners out here.

It meant they were about a mile from safety. Not too far. They could make it. Now the only hard part, discerning which way to go.

First things first, get to the clearing without catching on fire. Tony pulled Hope along; she was beginning to lose steam. He could tell the smoke was taking its toll on her. It was on him, as well.

Once they were in the middle of the clearing, Hope stopped. In between coughs she pleaded, "Please, I need to rest."

While Tony knew it was dangerous to stop, he also knew she needed a break. And this was the best spot to do it. He pulled out the water and handed her the bottle. This time, Hope took it greedily. And she drank it until he stopped her.

"Hope, you need to save some. We're close, but not yet there." He pulled the bottle from her and put it in his pack.

She plopped down on the dirt and Tony looked around at the fire. They still had a little time before it encircled them, but not much. He sat down next to her and took a drink from his bottle as well. "We can't sit long."

"I know. I'm just so tired." The coughing fit that wracked her body had Tony worried she'd die from smoke inhalation before the fire ever got to them.

He wasn't faring much better. Coughs overtook him, and even if he wanted, he couldn't have stood up at that moment. The idea that they may not make it past this clearing started to take root in his heart. He pulled her close to his body and held her tightly. "I'm so sorry."

"It's not your fault. You didn't know the winds had turned or that the fire had come this close. Neither of us did. I'm just sorry that I'm taking you down with me." In Hope's heart, she knew this was the end. She didn't have the strength to go on, and she doubted Tony would leave her, even if he could walk out of there.

Even though tears had been streaming down her cheeks for a while now due to the smoke, they began rushing as she thought about Tony dying. She wasn't worried about her death. She knew she'd fall asleep before the flames got to her. If what the movies said was true, she'd die from the smoke before her body burned. And by then, she'd be in Heaven with Jesus. It wouldn't be bad.

But she didn't want to leave her family and friends, not yet. And she wanted more time with Tony. All pretenses gone, she knew Tony was the one for her. Everything in her being said that once they were both ready for a relationship, it would happen.

However, that couldn't happen if they died.

And she didn't want Tony to survive a suicide bomber in the Middle East only to come home and die in a forest fire because she'd wanted to go to the back of the property and have a picnic. If she ever got out of this alive, she'd pay more attention to the fire warnings, and make sure that there was always a clear path to get back home. She'd probably start carrying an ax too. Or something to help clear brush in their path should she ever find herself near a fire again.

How could they have been so unobservant as to not realize that the fire was so close to them?

"Hey, do you think you can walk? There's still a little path ahead. You can make it if you hurry." Tony's words were beginning to slur, as though he were drunk, or falling asleep.

Hope worried for his safety. In that moment, she had a burst of energy. She wasn't going to let him die there. "Tony, let's go. Come on." She tried to stand, but her legs wouldn't allow it.

"I can't… You…go… Get to…safety." Tony was past coughing; he was barely speaking.

In that moment, Hope knew. She knew beyond a shadow of a doubt that it was over. And her heart broke. It broke for the family Tony wouldn't have. And for the memories they wouldn't be able to make together. Then she realized Tony didn't know how she felt. If this was the end, she wasn't going to go without telling him.

In a raspy voice that sounded like she was the world's worst chain-smoker, she began to open her heart. "Tony, stay with me for just a little while longer."

"Hmm. Yes." He nuzzled up closer to her and put his nose in her hair. He winced when all he got was a nose full of smoke. Then he moved his face closer to her neck. "Hope, I'm sorry."

Not wanting to let him go yet, she turned and put her hands on either side of his face. "Tony Sullivan, you open your eyes and look at me. Now."

He forced his eyes open. "Hope."

The sadness she saw there must have mirrored hers. But she wasn't going to let him go without the truth. "Tony, I lied to you."

His brows furrowed. He was about to say something but she cut him off.

"I don't want to be friends."

"What?" The sadness was replaced with hurt. "I'm sorry… I didn't mean…"

Hope cut him off again, trying to keep him from using the last of his energy. "I want more than friendship." She leaned in, and her lips met his in a soft kiss. Hope had intended to leave it at that, but something urged her to put more passion into it. She pressed her lips against his and wrapped her arms around his neck.

Tony didn't hesitate once he felt the urgency in her kiss. He dropped the blanket and put his arms around her. He held her tight, never wanting to let her go. If this was Heaven, he'd gladly take it.

The kiss deepened. Neither knew who instigated it, but both enjoyed it. Using up what they thought was the last of their strength and air, they kept their lips together.

Hope thought she'd never been happier. They were together. It might only be for a few more minutes, but she'd enter Heaven with joy in her heart. If they had to die, this was the best outcome she could have hoped for.

Even though the heat surrounding them was stifling, Tony's warmth enveloped her, and she leaned in as close to him as she could. Her coughing fit broke their kiss, but Tony still held her. When she was done coughing, she leaned her head against his chest.

"I'm glad we met, Hope. And if God somehow arranges for us to survive, I want more than friendship too." Tony took his time getting the words out. They were raspy and barely audible over the roar of the fire. It had completely surrounded them while they kissed, but he was content. More than content even if these were his last minutes.

Chapter 24

Tony caught himself drifting off, air barely coming and going in his smoke-filled lungs. Hope was quiet in his arms. They were past speaking. He knew neither had the air to get a word out. They had maybe minutes remaining with this life.

Praise God they had the next life to live. It wouldn't be the same; it would be better. He'd not be missing part of an ear, or have the scars of a beast on his face. Their earthly bodies would be replaced with perfect bodies in Heaven. They wouldn't ever be sick again. But they wouldn't have romantic love, either. That was the one thing he wished he had more time for, to love Hope the way she deserved.

But he'd not let his last few minutes go without showing her his love. Tony pulled her as close to his body as he could and leaned his head down to rest in the crook of her neck. It might not be comfortable for him, but when she sighed and snuggled up against him, he knew it was exactly what she wanted.

He was beyond tears, but if he had enough in him to cry, he would. He'd cry for the loss of Hope's life here on

Earth. He'd cry for the lost chance to marry her one day. But he wouldn't cry for them both joining Jesus in Heaven. That would be a wonderful gift.

But…

He wasn't ready to leave Hope here.

Father, if it's possible, please save us both. I look forward to the time I'll be in Heaven with you, I do. But there's something inside of me telling me that I have more to do here. And I don't think it's just Hope. Is there something you want me to do here? Do you have a calling for me on Earth still? I'll gladly do whatever you want if you'll save us. Either way, thank you for loving me. And thank you so much for the time I did have with Hope. It was a true gift. Amen.

Tony had heard many people say that before they died, their life flashed before their eyes. His didn't. Instead, he closed his eyes and let loose a breath.

Chapter 25

An annoying sound woke Hope from what she thought would be her death. If this was death, she wanted none of it. Her throat hurt, her eyes were so sore she couldn't open them, and the sound… It hurt. In fact, her entire body hurt.

Would she have to feel the flames surrounding her as she died? Shouldn't she have passed quietly from smoke inhalation? But that noise. What was it? It sounded familiar, but far away.

Then another sound soothed her soul. It was low, and hoarse, but she knew she liked it. And before she knew it, that other sound drowned out the good one. "No," she rasped. She wanted the good sound again.

"Hope. Wake up." Tony's hoarse voice sounded again, this time right in her ear.

"Tony?" She tried to open her eyes, but they burned so badly. Had the fire burned her eyes out? No, she wasn't on fire. She was hot. Hotter than she'd ever been. But there was a fan above her. Someone was fanning her.

"We're saved… Helicopter." While Tony couldn't get all the words out, Hope knew what he was saying.

The fan above her was the blades of a helicopter, there to save them from the fire.

Either that, or this was a really unfair dream.

Hope reached her hand out to Tony, and he took it.

"You first." Tony wrapped something around her.

"No…you…first," she hacked out between coughs.

It was too late; she felt herself being lifted on a breeze, and when she no longer felt Tony close, she managed to squint one eye open enough to see that she was several feet above him, and rising. A small smile played on his face as he laid back in the dirt and watched her go.

As she rose in the air, she could see the flames surrounding their spot had begun to die down. The trees around them were burnt, and mostly gone. How long had they slept there in the little clearing? It must have been hours.

"Miss, miss. Can you hear me?" A foreign voice yelled at her over the sound of chopper blades slicing through the sky.

She tried to say yes, but nothing came out. She nodded, and a mask went over her face before she was fully inside the helicopter. She tried to take it off and ask about Tony, but she was too weak to bring her hand to her mouth. Instead, she fell back into oblivion.

When she did wake up again, it was to an insistent beeping noise that caused her head to pound. Hope could have sworn someone was trying to pull her head apart.

She blinked her eyes, and the bright lights hurt almost as much as the smoke had. She closed them again.

"Hope, are you awake?" A voice she knew better than her own sounded close to her.

"Dana?" she whispered and realized she could talk. Not much, but she knew it was enough when a soft hand squeezed hers.

"Yes, I'm here. You're safe. And you're going to be alright." A sob escaped her cousin.

Hope worked her eyes and cracked them open just a bit. "Tony? Did he?" She couldn't bring herself to say the words.

"Yes, he's alive. And doing well. He's in the room next to yours." A manly voice assured her. He sounded strained, as if he was fighting back tears.

"Jerod?"

"Yes, we're all here," Jerod answered.

"The ranch?"

Dana chuckled, and if Hope wasn't mistaken, she did it while tears streamed down her face. Hope tried to put a hand up, but she was too weak.

"Don't worry. The ranch was saved. And before you ask, all of the animals were too. A few were singed a bit, and some needed oxygen, but all are going to make it." Dana couldn't say more before she began sobbing. "I'm just so glad you survived."

"Me, too." And Hope fell asleep with a tiny smile on her face.

The next time Hope woke up, she was able to open her eyes, and the throbbing pain in her head was gone.

"Hope? Can you hear me?" That familiar raspy voice sent thrills though her body.

"Tony? Oh, Tony." Hope turned her whole body to get a better look at him. "You're alright?"

"Yes, I'm better than alright, now that you're awake." He leaned down and kissed her forehead.

"We made it? Really?" When she felt tears pricking the backs of her eyes, she let them flow.

"We did."

Chapter 26

It took a few days before they were both back home.
And a few weeks before either was up and about as
usual. But Hope and Tony made a full recovery. In fact,
they were meeting up at the coffee shop in town for
Saturday Pancake Day.

"I can't believe how much everything has changed in
the past few weeks," Hope said before taking a bite of her
chocolate chip pancakes.

"I'm just glad God saw fit to give us another chance
here on Earth, together." Tony took one of Hope's hands
and squeezed it.

She gazed into his eyes. "Me, too."

"Oh, come on. Get a room." Skeeter gagged and rolled
his eyes. But then he laughed. He had been to the hospital
every day to visit them both. And then when Hope was
sent home, he came over to see her everyday as well. He
even brought her coffee and contraband chocolate a few
times.

Her doctor had said to stay away from sugar, but there
was no way Hope was going to do that. And Skeeter

understood. He had actually been a real help to both Hope and Tony as they had recovered.

"Skeeter, you know you're just jealous she chose me over you." Tony winked at Hope, then turned to grin at his friend.

"Yeah, yeah." He waved a hand. "Just keep that mushy stuff to yourselves."

"What mushy stuff? We didn't even kiss." Hope complained. She wanted a kiss, badly.

However, just the evening before she and Tony had a long talk. While they were moving forward with a romantic relationship, they were going to take it slowly. That meant not being alone with each other too much. And keeping their kisses appropriate. As it turned out, Hope wasn't the only one who hadn't waited for marriage. And Tony wanted them to wait now.

Hope agreed.

They both still had a lot of healing to do, but she also knew they would do it together. God had given them a new life. One neither was going to squander.

"So, tell me about the new woman at the ranch." Hope turned her gaze to Skeeter, knowing that he'd be crushing on anyone with two X chromosomes.

The young cowboy turned his face down, but Hope caught the pink on his cheeks. Yup, Skeeter was smitten. She wasn't surprised.

Skeeter cleared his throat. "So, Tony, you said you had some ideas for the ranch? Have you spoken to Jerod yet?"

Tony chuckled, knowing that Skeeter was trying to change the subject. Poor kid. He'd be cool and give him a break. Especially since he'd turned his attention away from

Hope. Not that Tony thought he had any real competition, but it did irk him at times the way he and Hope joked and laughed.

"We did. Once the fire damage on the land is all cleaned up, we're gonna look for some cuddling cows. And I think you said you would work with us all on how to make a few things from wood?" Tony arched a brow. After the fire, Skeeter suggested they take the useable wood that was chopped down in an effort to stop the fire, and use it to make carvings they could sell at the various events throughout the year. The Big Sky Christmas Tree Farm owner, Cody, had told them they could have a booth any time they wanted. And for free too.

Dana and Hope both suggested a few other items to add, and if they could get it going, they'd have enough product in stock by Christmas.

Even Megan had already started making afghans to sell. And she'd taught Mike how to crochet.

Tony was amazed at all that had happened while he was healing up. His final surgery was scheduled for next week, and the doctor told him he should be healed up enough by the middle of November to enjoy the seasonal festivities.

"I did. Have you ever whittled?" All blushing aside, Skeeter was down to business.

"A little, but not much. And I'm not very good at it. I'd do better cutting the wood or sanding it for the final touches." The last time Tony had tried to make a small horse, it'd looked more like the Creature from the Black Lagoon. He just couldn't seem to get the wood to bend to what he imagined in his tiny brain.

Buffy sat at Tony's feet, being quiet. But before Tony noticed anything, she nudged his left leg. By now, he knew exactly what that meant. He turned, prepared for anything, but smiled when he saw Cody coming toward them with a full platter of fresh cinnamon rolls and coffee cakes.

"Howdy, neighbors. It sure is good to see you both out and about again. How ya feeling?" Cody, the owner of the Big Sky Christmas Tree Farm, put the plate of sugary goodness down in the middle. "Help yourselves."

Hope smiled and thanked Cody for his generosity. Once the pleasantries were out of the way, she wanted to know what he had planned for the fall festival.

"Well, if I told you…" He let the joke trail off and chuckled. "Actually, I don't know everything we're doing yet. Sadie will have to be the one to ask. She tells me what to do, and I do it."

"No questions asked, right?" Jerod teased.

"You got it. I know better than to second-guess the woman who saved my family farm. Any plan she has is one that I want to do." Cody nodded once, then leaned in to grab one of the coffee cakes to go with his cup of joe.

Hope looked around. "Where's Sadie?"

"Oh, you know." Cody puffed his chest out and sat taller in his seat.

Confusion marred Hope's face, and she shook her head.

"You haven't heard? I thought that news had made its way around town already." Cody chuckled and wiped his face. "While you were in the hospital, I asked her to marry me."

"And she said yes?" Skeeter's incredulous tone belied his happiness for the couple.

"Hey now," Cody chuffed.

With a good-natured chuckle, Skeeter admitted he was happy for the couple. "I actually thought you'd do it sooner. When you gettin' hitched?"

Cody sat back in his chair, pride deflating before everyone's eyes. "You know, I don't know. Sadie took off yesterday with her best friend to check out wedding gowns in Seattle. They'll be gone for a few days."

Hope opened her mouth, then closed it. Then she opened it again. "I bet that if she's already looking at gowns, it means she's planning to marry you soon. When she gets back you should ask her when she wants to do it."

"A Christmas wedding would be fun." Skeeter grinned and bit off a bit of cinnamon roll.

Cody shook his head. "No, not Christmas. It's too busy. I bet she'd want a spring wedding."

"Did I hear someone say a spring wedding?" Jessica Lambton, affectionately known as Mrs. Claus come the Christmas season, smiled when she walked up to the table. And behind her was Christopher Lambton, her husband and Santa Claus.

"Jessica. It's so good to see you." Cody stood up. "Chris, are you getting ready?" He put his hand out, and the older gentleman shook it with vigor.

"I'm more interested in this wedding business of yours." Christopher put his arm around his wife and nodded to everyone at the table. "We could use a large wedding to boost morale around here."

"Are you talking about the Hendersons?" Lottie walked up with the coffee order for the Lambtons.

"Such a sad business. Losing their entire farm to the fire. And all their stock, too." Jessica's frown mirrored everyone else's.

Hope had heard about the loss when she'd gotten back to her aunt and uncle's place after her hospital stay. Thankfully, their ranch wasn't touched. But the Henderson's, they had a large farm that had been completely decimated by the fire. And their stock… Well, none of them survived. The fire came upon them too quickly to do anything but save the lives of the family.

"Does anyone know what they're going to do?" Hope hadn't heard anything more and didn't even know where the family was staying.

"They're staying out with the Martinez family for now. But they aren't sure they want to rebuild once they get the check from the insurance company." Chris had been out to see them on several occasions, and even offered to help rebuild.

"I think we should try to find a way to make this Christmas special for them. Especially for their kids." Jessica always did something special for families in need at Christmas. Children were so near and dear to her heart.

"I'd like to help." Hope had been looking for some way to give back. God had done so much for her lately. She was confident he'd forgiven her for Billy. And the fact he'd sent a helicopter in to save her and Tony before it was too late only cemented her need to do something for others.

"Aren't you a doll." Jessica beamed at Hope. They didn't know each other well, but Hope had been around Frenchtown enough to know exactly who Mrs. Claus was.

She'd always wanted to get to know the woman more. And it seemed she was going to get her chance.

"Why don't we get together the beginning of next week. We can discuss things we can do now to help the family. I was thinking we could start a clothes drive. They have a few things that were given to them by the Martinez family, and a few others in the area, but I know they need more. Especially with the cold winter just around the corner." If Jessica had her way, every family in the region would help out.

"I know I have a few things I haven't really worn yet, and most likely won't." Hope bit her lip and looked to Jerod and Dana. Dana's parents had given Hope a couple of items last Christmas that she really didn't care for. They were nice, just not Hope's style. Maybe Mrs. Martinez would like them. Either way, she'd do whatever she could to help.

"You are so sweet. Are you sure you're up to helping? I don't want you to have any setbacks in your healing." Jessica put a hand over her heart.

While Hope wasn't back to her normal self yet, she was itching to get out there and do more. Her aunt and uncle didn't let her work more than an hour in the morning and then an hour in the afternoon. Her breathing wasn't one hundred percent yet, but each day she had more strength than the day before, and she needed to get out of the house. She was going to go stir-crazy if she didn't.

"Why don't you bring the kids over to the Crooked Arrow later this week? I bet Mike would love to share his cows with the kids, and maybe even teach them how to churn butter. And then I can take them for a short ride, if they like." Tony had been itching to do more as well. Ever since he saw that helicopter, he knew God had more for him to do. And he wasn't about to shirk his responsibility.

It went deeper than responsibility. Tony knew he had an assignment from God. While he may not know all the details, he did know that the Man Upstairs still had plans for him down here.

And he was ready to head the call.

Epilogue

Tony's surgery went off without a hitch. When Tony woke up, the doctors were smiling.

"When do the bandages come off?" Tony was ready for the next stage in his life, but first he had to get past this last hurdle.

"In a couple of days," Doctor Bailey informed him.

For the next week, Tony did everything the doctors and nurses told him to do. He even ate the green vegetables on his plate, something he really didn't care for. But he was anxious to get out and for his body to complete the healing process.

"So, Doc. What's my prognosis?" It was the day before he was scheduled to head home. The VA had paid to send him to a world-renowned surgeon who specialized in burn victims.

"While I don't see you ever hearing again from your left ear—though I have seen miracles happen before—I do think the side of your face will have minimal scars. Most people won't even be able to tell."

The doctor never promised his skin would be perfect, but from the sounds of it, things were going to be better than he had hoped.

"So, no bionic ear?" While Tony had been in the hospital recovering, he'd watched several hours of TV a day. One of his favorite shows was from the seventies. The Six Million Dollar Man was a show about a former astronaut who had to have so much reconstructive surgery, he was considered bionic.

Tony wouldn't mind having bionic hearing. That could be useful when it came to dealing with the guys at the ranch, and their practical jokes. It seemed Skeeter was up to no good lately. But in reality, it was probably a good thing for everyone to laugh.

Since Tony had been in the LA hospital, he hadn't seen Hope. But they did have nightly calls once he was cognizant enough to speak on the phone. She told him about Skeeter's version of a bug prank. Skeeter had cut out shapes of different bugs and spiders and taped them to the inside of the lampshades. The first time Dana turned on a lamp, she jumped in shock. Tony was a little proud of the guy for such a great prank. But he missed being there to see it for himself.

More than that, he missed Hope. Tony was looking forward to seeing her at the airport. She promised she would be there to pick him up and take him home.

So when his plane arrived, and he saw her, he missed everything else. That is, until the sounds reached his ear.

"Welcome home!" Multiple loud voices shouted over the din of the Kalispel airport.

When Tony first walked into the small terminal, he only had eyes for Hope. Her big smile, and the excitement that shone in her eyes, had him under a spell.

Then, when he realized that practically the entire town was there to greet him, his smile faltered. But only for a moment. He rallied and looked at all the people he knew. Then, he saw Buffy. Nelly was holding her by her leash, but the dog strained at her collar to get to him.

No matter how much he wanted to greet Hope first, he knew if he didn't get to Buffy first, he'd hurt her feelings. As a kid, he had a dog. And when he came home from college the first time, he waited to greet his dog last. Big mistake. She had ignored him for most of the weekend. Tony wasn't going to do that to Buffy.

"Buffy, my girl." Tony knelt down and rubbed the dog's head. "I've missed you."

The dog pulled enough on her leash to lean closer and lick his face.

"Buffy," Nelly exclaimed. "I taught you better than that."

Tony didn't mind. He wrapped his arms around her neck and hugged her. "Good to see you, girl." Then he stood and pulled Hope into his arms.

"Whoa now. You just let another girl kiss you before you kissed me. I think you have to go wash your face first, mister." Hope pulled back, but only a little.

Tony took that as a sign she was joking and gave her light kiss on the lips. His real greeting could wait until they were alone.

And what a greeting it was.

Hope drove them back to the ranch with Buffy in the cab of her truck. The dog had refused to go back with anyone but Tony.

"I'm so glad to see you. You should know, there's a big party waiting for you at the ranch. Everyone missed you. But I don't think anyone did as much as I did." Hope looked over at Tony sitting in the passenger seat. She took his hand in hers for a moment and squeezed it.

Buffy chuffed, reminding them both that she was there and had missed her partner, too.

"Yes, I know you missed him." Hope looked in her rearview mirror at Buffy, who returned the look.

As they pulled into the drive of the Crooked Arrow Ranch, Tony put his hand on hers. "Can we stop before we get to the house? I want to give you something before everyone joins us."

"Sure thing, but you don't have to give me anything." Unsure what he would have gotten her, she pulled to the side of the drive.

"Let's get out, just you and I." Tony looked at Buffy and commanded, "*Bleib*," or stay. He didn't want Buffy joining him on this mission.

Tony walked around the truck to join Hope at the tailgate. "I really missed you." Not giving her a chance to speak, he pulled her to him and kissed her.

When their lips met, a fire deep within him stirred. One he never wanted to extinguish. All too soon, he had to slow the kiss and pull away. Just as he was about to, a horn honked. Then it kept honking.

Thinking someone was driving up, Tony pulled back. He touched his forehead to hers. Hope's breathing was just as heavy as his. When he heard the sound again, he pulled back and looked around. But no one was nearby. Then he looked inside the cab and noticed that Buffy was in the driver's seat, paws on the steering wheel right where the horn was.

"Oh, Buffy!" they exclaimed in unison.

So, what did you think? Are you loving the way the service dogs interact with their partners? Do you think dogs really are that smart? I tell you; they are. All of the dogs that have been part of my family over the years do some of the quirky things I've written down. In fact, my mom's dog that is currently staying with me, loves to herd me toward the cabinet with the treats. LOL He comes and gets me, then he guides me toward the kitchen. There is one step down along the way, and he ALWAYS stops right there and makes sure I see it. Then, he will go forward and let me follow him to the treats. Frankie makes me laugh all the time.

And when he wants to go outside, he guides me to the front door. While writing this book, the weather went back and forth between really cold and so-so. When it was really cold, I'd put Frankie's Carhart jacket on him. Let me tell you, the dog knew he was hot! He pranced around for all to see him in his most handsome jacket. There were even a few times I had to chase him around the house to get the jacket off once we were back inside. Aren't dogs awesome?

Tony's past experience when he forgot to say hi to his childhood dog first is a true story. I lived with my aunt and uncle for a while. Then when I moved away to attend college, I'd come back and visit on occasion. One time, Frannie (my aunt's dog), came to the door and wanted me to greet her first. I greeted her last. And let me tell you, she did not let me forget. She gave me the cold shoulder the rest of that trip. And from then on out, everyone knew that I had to greet Frannie before I could say anything to them. It became a thing. Even my cousin would ask if I'd said hi to Frannie before I could get a hug from her. LOL

I'm gonna post some pics of Frankie in his stylish duds on Facebook. So if you have a FB account, check me out. My links are in the pages to come, so keep reading. And share pictures on the post of your animals. Especially if they have any clothes or toys that they have to show off whenever they can.

And don't forget to check out book 3, Love's Healing Balm. This one is going to be my most personal story yet.

While this is all fiction, there are some parts that a writer always uses that comes from real life. They say write what you know. I'm a US Army veteran who was injured during service. I'm currently 40% disabled. I don't need a service dog. I never saw combat, but I did serve during Desert Storm and have friends who did see combat, some who never returned home. And too many to name who have mental and physical challenges that require love, patience, and understanding.

I know that a lot of you understand this. I've heard from so many of you who have either served or have a loved one who has served. Thank you to all of our servicemembers and their family and friends who support them! It can be tough to support someone who has been severely injured. But just think what their life would be like if their family and friends turned their backs on them.

The Crooked Arrow Ranch is a made-up place. However, Frenchtown Montana is real. I made a few modifications to the area, but for the most part it's very close. And there are a lot of services available to help those who served, as well as those who care for a servicemember. Please check with your local VA and find out about the various free services or discounts available today.

Organizations like Wounded Warrior project exist just to help our veterans. And there are groups that take veterans, and even their spouses, out on trips. Sometimes it's just camping. Other trips involve fishing or hunting. And cow cuddling is real y'all. Look it up.

Contact Me

For those of you who love social media, here are the various ways to follow or contact me:

BookBub: https://www.bookbub.com/authors/jenna-hendricks
Instagram: https://www.instagram.com/j.l.hendricks/
Twitter: https://twitter.com/TinkFan25
Facebook: https://www.facebook.com/JLHendricksAuthor
Website: https://jennahendricks.com

Free Short Story

Free short story when you join my newsletter
See how Jerod and Dana met and fell in love today!
https://jennahendricks.com/newsletter/

Wounded Hearts
Ranch
A Big Sky
Novella
CROOKED ARROW RANCH
CROOKED ARROW
RANCH
JENNA HENDRICKS